Ian Cochrane was born in 1941 and grew up in the village of Cullybackey in County Antrim. He was educated by R.L. Russell, an advocate of progressive education, who encouraged his pupils to create art from their own experience.

Ian began his working life aged 14 in a local linen mill but soon afterwards he began to lose his vision. After adapting to life with limited sight he moved to London in 1959 and, initially, worked as a piano tuner. Over the following years he would hold many jobs, as a lift attendant, a civil servant, a drugs counsellor, and a creative writing teacher. However, after being approached by Faber & Faber, who were interested in his short stories, he became a full-time writer.

His first novel, *A Streak of Madness*, was published in 1973 while his second, *Gone in the Head*, was a runner-up in the 1974 Guardian Fiction Prize. His first novels drew on his experiences growing up in Northern Ireland while his later work portrayed the similarly anarchic life of young men in west London. His last novel, *The Slipstream*, was published in 1983.

In 1987 he was brutally beaten up and suffered from his injuries for many years. Despite suffering from increasing blindness in his later years, Cochrane remained a distinctive presence on the London literary scene.

Ian Cochrane died in 2004.

[illegible] was born in 1941 and grew up in the [illegible]

[illegible]

[illegible] writer.

[illegible]

The Last Word

Selected Short Stories

Ian Cochrane

Edited by Philip Taylor

turnpike books

First published in Great Britain by Turnpike Books

turnpikebooks@gmail.com

ISBN 9781916254763

Our House, *The Green* Door, *The Last Word* and *The Big Ginger Cat* were first published in 'Introduction 4' (Faber and Faber, 1970); *You Can't Buy It* and *Hell Will Never Be Full* were first published in 'Penguin Modern Stories 12' (1972); *The Wet Eye* was first published in 'Best Irish Short Stories', edited by David Marcus (1975). *The Gravedigger* was first published in 'More Magazine' (1975). *Mad Peter* was first published in 'Aquarius Magazine' (1972).

Jennings Talks to ... Ian Cochrane was first published in 'Jennings Magazine' (1985).

Printed and bound by
Clays Ltd, Elcograf S.p.A.

CONTENTS

FOREWORD

For close on thirty years, I considered Ian Cochrane to be my dearest, best friend, and it was only when I came to write his obituary in 2004 that it became obvious many others who knew him also laid claim to that privilege. However, my own first encounter with "the wee man" was in the late sixties when I travelled over from Belfast to record a BBC radio documentary on a new wave of Ulster-born people beginning to make a name for themselves in the arts in the capital at that time.

We met at his flat – well, more realistically, I suppose, a bed-sit – in a house near the Bayswater Road he shared with several other like-minded, bohemian types. As though born into that particular lifestyle, Ian was naturally drawn in that direction, even early on in his home village of Cullybackey.

We went to lunch in a Greek restaurant close by, our friendship sealed over several bottles of retsina and glasses of ouzo. So much so I overstayed my official remit by a further week spent in his company. Sharing the same Antrim mill-village background, we had a common identity as well as dialect, which caused much bemusement in Ian's local just as it did in the wider reaches of the London literary scene later on.

Our meeting place was the Churchill Arms in Kensington Church Street, very much a "Paddy pub" back then, where, perched on his stool at the bar, Ian would sing Orange songs whilst I hovered in the background. And even today, after all this time, Ian's memory lives on inside in the form of a polished brass plaque above the stool he made his own.

In 1970 I came to work and live in the capital myself, not all that many bus stops from his new address in Saint Stephen's Gardens, close to Notting Hill, which along with Soho and the King's Road in Chelsea was the cultural epicentre of everything happening then in Swinging London.

Meeting up once, often twice a week, our afternoon routine became fixed. Coffee and cakes and talk about almost everything save our own work, which curiously enough had become this taboo subject as though we were both wary of encroaching on one another's territory even though our writing had long since moved in different directions. Looking back, I suppose one could say it was a sort of good-hearted literary rivalry between the two of us. Ian was given to boasting that, of course, he happened to be the more "authentic" writer, while ignoring the fact that I was the one who'd won the Guardian Fiction prize in 1969 and he was a runner-up five years later.

And so, after finishing his double espresso and one last cigarette, he'd go back to his top-floor flat to watch *Columbo*, as nothing would make him miss a single episode of the series. I often suspect he may have felt some kind of secret affinity with that short-sighted, cigar-smoking, bumbling TV detective in his bedraggled raincoat.

At that time the authors we both admired and discussed endlessly were William Faulkner, Flannery O'Connor, Truman Capote and Eudora Welty, all from the American Deep South of course. Perhaps, we recognised a connection there as being a couple of Scotch-Irish rednecks ourselves. Also, I recall, Ian loved and often quoted from the Uncle Remus Tar-Baby stories set in that same part of the States.

When we felt it necessary to get away from London, particularly when the Notting Hill Carnival took over the streets outside Ian's flat over one intolerably disruptive and noisy August weekend, we would take off together, not just on trips to places like Bristol, York or Norwich, but also across the Channel to Boulogne and Bruges. Usually, however, we'd simply take the train down to Kent to the village of Goodnestone where Ian and his wife Maggie had lived for a time. And even in that most English of hamlets, the locals there still saw Ian as this officially sanctioned character holding court in the FitzWalter Arms whenever he happened to make a return visit to the place.

A favourite story they told in the pub was about one fierce winter when he'd been snowed in up at the big FitzWalter house, where he and Maggie had their flat. Desperate to make his way to the pub, getting into his wife's car, and despite being partially sighted, plus of course unable and unauthorised to drive, setting off regardless, he'd ended up crashing into a tree, luckily only damaging the car but not himself.

But then despite being roughly five foot three and outwardly puny in appearance, Ian was self-confident and fearless to an almost worrying degree, never shying away from any sort of a scrimmage, verbal or physical. He was instantly recognisable on the streets of West London in his long flowing woollen scarf and child-sized sailor's cap, nimble and neat-footed in those flamenco dancer shoes of his.

To those of us still around who so loved being his company, we still cherish memories of the little man on his stool at the bar with a pint in his hand, who made every occasion joyous with his sayings and droll, salty take on life. Luckily, for a younger generation missing out on those occasions, his personality lives on in his novels and short stories, like those in this collection.

Maurice Leitch

THE WET EYE

Ma hit me for dirting my face, and I left home straight away. No, that's a lie, I got ready for Sunday school first. But all the time I was getting ready I had it in my head to run away and I did. I never got to Sunday school. Maybe I knew from last week I was going to run away because I hadn't even learnt the verse I was supposed to learn. Anyway it was time I left home because Ma was getting on my nerves. If I wasn't dirty she said it wouldn't be long before I was, and if I *was* dirty then she hit me. She hit me any chance she got. She hit me if I wet my hands, she hit me if I scratched my knee and she hit me if I tried to ride Da's bicycle and got grease on my leg. She hit me too if I threw a bit of bread to the hens, and she hit me if I wasn't feeling too well and couldn't go to school. She hit me if somebody else fought with me or if I cried. She hit me if I ate too much and she hit me if I didn't eat enough. She hit me if I climbed a tree and she hit me if I didn't go out to play. She hit me if I kept quiet because she thought I had done something wrong and she hit me if I was noisy.

When I ran away I went to Uncle Robert's because I knew he wouldn't hit me. I told him about Ma hitting me and he listened. Then he took a big deep breath and never breathed out again for a long time. I just sat there with him in front of the fire and watched him thinking.

After a while he says, 'There's one thing you've got to learn.'

'What's that?' I ask.

'Never trust a woman,' he says. I said I would remember that, and that was it settled. I was going to stay with him.

We sat in front of the fire and Uncle chewed tobacco slow and I knew there was something going round in his mind. For a bit I thought maybe he didn't want me, but then he says, 'If you're going to live here, we've got to eat.'

He chewed his tobacco slow for a long time. Then he says, 'We've got to sow the land.'

'What land?' I ask. Because I know that Uncle has no land except for a couple of yards in front of the house and a couple of yards at the back, and it was in pretty bad shape. It was just nettles, briars and stones and a few tin cans and barrel hoops. He looked a bit hurt when I said, 'What land,' and I didn't know what to say.

'My land,' he says, and I said nothing. Then we started talking about it and I forgot about the size of it. We were going to plant apple trees and plum trees and keep the hens for the eggs and maybe a cow for the milk. And we were going to plant all sorts of vegetables and everything. We talked and talked about our plans and we went to bed and talked about them. And next morning we got up and we were still talking about them. We talked about our plans until lunch time and then we went to the pub and we still talked. Uncle didn't ask me if I drank. He just went up to the bar and came back with two pints. I tasted it and twisted up my face.

'It puts lead in your pencil,' he says. 'It makes your toes open and close with a bang.' Then I drank it slow like him.

'First things first,' he says. And I wondered what he meant. He chewed his tobacco and nearly finished his pint before he said any more. Then he says, 'We need a spade and a hook.'

'Is the hook for clearing the nettles?' I asked him. He looks at me as if I was a genius or something.

'That's right, that's right,' he says.

There's one thing I learnt from Uncle that day. That is not to rush things. I says we better get back and get stuck in, and he just says, 'Never walk before you can crawl.'

'Will we have to buy a spade?' I say.

'We'll cross that bridge when we come to it,' he says. 'I'll have a look in the shed to see what I've got.' Uncle had no idea what he had got in the shed.

That day I only had the one pint. He said it was enough for me to start off with. He had five or six. After he had about three, he started to talk about his land again. If there wasn't a spade and a hook in the shed he knew where he could borrow them. It was a chap that drank with him sometimes. Uncle had known him for thirty years. One time he came to Uncle when he had a broken chain on his bicycle and he had to go to a funeral the next day, and even though it was late, Uncle put the chain together and wouldn't take any money for it because he was going to a funeral. The man never forgot about this and every time he saw Uncle Robert in the pub he would buy him a pint. But they never got even because Uncle always bought him one back. So the man told him that if ever he could do anything for him he would. So Uncle told him that he might be able to help him some day. Now the time had come.

Uncle said we would have one for the road and we had two and then we went to see the man. We had to walk a long way across the fields. The man lived in a little hut much the same as Uncle's – with a big shed beside it. Uncle forgot to look in his shed and he told the man that if he found out that he had a spade and hook he would bring his straight back. The man was a thin man and his name was James. He smoked a pipe and he had the top of a pepper box stuck over the bowl to keep the ash from falling out. His house smelt of soap and polish. It was cleaner than Uncle's too. Uncle went straight in and told him that he was going to work his little bit of land and James says straight away, 'Well, if there's anything I can do.' And Uncle says, as if he had just thought about it, 'Well, while I'm here, come to think about it, there is.'

Then he told James what he wanted and James went straight out and threw the shed door open and told Uncle to take what he wanted. Uncle says he would only have the spade and hook, and James insisted that he have a shovel too, but Uncle wouldn't hear of it. All he had come for was the spade and hook and he was taking nothing else. They had a bit of an argument about it. Uncle said that he would bring the spade and hook back as soon as he was finished with them, and James said there was no hurry for them and Uncle says that he wouldn't keep anything longer than necessary – that he would be straight over with them on the same day as he had finished, and James says to Uncle that if he didn't stop talking like that he would hit him. Uncle says that if there was one thing he wouldn't do, that is fight with a friend. Uncle says he would rather come to James to borrow something than to a relation. James agreed. He said he never asked a relation for nothing and Uncle said neither did he. Then James insisted that Uncle come in and have a cup of tea. Uncle said no, that he would get back and get started. But it was no good. James pretended to be offended, and Uncle didn't want to hurt him so we had to go in.

The kettle was singing on the big black stove and a big black cat was lying curled up on a chair and it was purring loud. Uncle was going to sit down then he saw the cat and said he would stand. But James wouldn't hear of that. He pushed the cat off the chair and made Uncle sit down. I sat on a little stool. James went down into a little room and back and slipped a round white peppermint into my hand and winked at me as much as to say, not to tell Uncle. Uncle pretended not to see and I slipped it into my mouth.

James kept his pipe in his mouth all the time. Even when he was talking. He had a white shirt on too. It was nice and clean and it had a stud in the neck but no collar. Every now and then he would put his hand up to his neck as if he thought there was a tie there. Uncle looked all around the room and looked as if he wanted to say something but couldn't think what. Then he looked out the window.

'It's not a bad day,' he says.

'No,' James says, 'it's not. I wouldn't mind if it stayed like this – I wouldn't mind if it stayed like this the whole year round.' Uncle agreed with him, and said that he didn't like it if it was too hot either. James said that he didn't know who was tampering with the weather, but it wasn't as good as it was. You couldn't tell the difference between winter and summer. Uncle said that nature wasn't to be tampered with. Then Uncle went on again about the spade and hook. He would bring it back as soon as he had finished. Uncle never brought anything back he borrowed – he was known for that. Folk said that Uncle would never ask anybody to buy his pint for him but never to lend him anything. Uncle told James about the time he lent a man a hammer and he never brought it back. He said he held nothing against the man, but he would never lend him anything again. Then James told about the time he lent a man a pound and he was a very wealthy man, but he never paid it back. After that we set off for home. I carried the hook and Uncle carried the spade. He carried it over his shoulder and he looked just like a man coming home from work.

We were just coming up to Uncle's house when we saw Da standing at the door. We both stopped, but it was too late, Da had seen us.

'You'll not let him take me back,' I say to Uncle.

'Oh, no,' he says and walks straight on with the spade over his shoulder and his chin shot out.

'I can't go back anyway,' I say. 'We have all that work to do. It'll take us a while getting that land ready.'

Da had one hand in his pocket and he didn't look too upset.

'Do you want something?' Uncle says when we got up to him.

Da didn't answer him. He just looked at me.

'Are you coming or staying?' he says.

'Staying,' I say and he just walks away. He doesn't walk quick – he just walks at his ease. Uncle puts the spade to the ground and leans on it and watches Da walking away. Then when he has gone out of sight Uncle looks at me and takes a big deep breath.

'Do you want to stay or go?' he says.

'Stay,' I say. Uncle brings out his handkerchief and wipes his brow and then looks to see how much sweat is on it.

'That was a near thing,' he says. Then we go and put the hook and spade in the shed and bar the door.

'Are we not going to start on that bit of land?' I say.

'Never run before you can walk,' he says.

We looked at the couple of yards at the front of the house, then we went round and looked at the couple of yards at the back. Then we went inside. Uncle says nothing for a while. He just went down into the bedroom and starts taking off his clothes. I didn't know what to say, so I just started taking off my clothes too. He got into bed and I got in too. We both lay on our backs. Then Uncle groped under the bed and brought out a lemonade bottle full of still. He drank some of the still laying on his back.

The bedroom smelt of cold for a while, then when Uncle had breathed in it for a while it got warmer. And the bed felt warmer too. Uncle was halfway down the bottle before he started talking.

'Oh, it's lovely stuff,' he says, and licked his wet lips. Then he starts singing.

I'm a rambler, I'm a gambler
I'm a long way from home
And if you don't like me
Just leave me alone
I'll eat when I'm hungry
And I'll drink when I'm dry
And if moonshine don't kill me
I'll live till I die.

Then he looks at me. 'I used to be a tramp,' he says. I turned around and listened to him.

'Oh, I was. I used to walk the road in the spring mornings. The grass was wet and green, and I didn't have a problem in my mind. I loved the spring sky. I would sing to myself and walk at my leisure. At night I would lie and sing under the sky. In the morning I would be glad to see the new day. And I would thank God that there was no woman to follow me. You can't live with a woman. You can't get on with them. You have to take your own road and leave them behind.'

'I think you're right,' I say.

'I'm right all right,' he says. 'I had a woman once. Yes, I met her on my travels. She took me in and fed me and gave me a bed to sleep in. I thought I was happy at first. Then something happened.'

'What?' I ask him. He stuck his leg out of the bed and pointed to his feet.

'Them,' he says. 'I got itchy feet.' He put his leg back into the bed and drank a bit more still. Then he went on, 'I told her that I had to get on the road and she went mad. She shouted at me and started tearing her hair out. She pulled it out in big handfuls and threw it on the ground. She stamped her feet till there was no soles in her shoes. She bit her nails till there was nothing left, only little stumps of fingers. She screamed till she burst her ears and she cried like a child.'

'What did you do?' I ask.

'I hit her and left,' he says. 'No, that was the end of that.'

Then he looks at me.

'Never get caught,' he says and he closed his eyes and kept on talking. 'In my travels one night I came across a little fire in the dark. I sat down and warmed my feet.'

Then there was a loud knock on the door. Uncle opened his eyes and then closed them again.

'Who is it?' he says.

'I'm not sure,' I say and we both lay still. Then the door got another loud bang. Uncle got up slow and went and looked out the window. Then he came back and got into bed. He didn't bother to say who it was and I didn't ask him. The door got another bang and I went to the window. It was Ma. I went and got into bed beside Uncle. Then Ma starts shouting in the door.

'I know you're in,' she shouts, 'I can smell you.'

'That's women for you,' Uncle shouts. 'They can't let sleeping dogs lie.'

'You lazy bugger,' Ma shouts.

'Does she mean you or me?' I say to Uncle. He took a big swig from the bottle and let his lips stay wet and closed his eyes.

'Does it matter?' he says. Ma must have been kicking the door now and she was shouting loud too.

'I'll report you to the authorities,' she shouts. 'You dirty big bugger. You got no right to him. He's only an innocent child. If he would stay at home and go to school and get something into his thick head. He learns nothing. I'll report you. You never were no good. You're a tramp – a dirty tramp. I sent him and he done nothing, but I'll do something. I'll report you. Is there something wrong with your head, or do you just like little boys?' Then she put on a kind of girlish voice. 'Do you just like little boys? Maybe you like little boys better than women. Maybe you need your head examined.' Uncle opened his eyes as if he was surprised that she was still at the door – as if he had been sleeping.

'Go home,' he shouts and closed his eyes again. His lips were still wet from the still. It sounded like Ma had gone. There was no noise for a long time.

'Maybe she won't come back again?' I say.

'If she's away,' Uncle says. Then there was a merciful scream at the window like a wild cat.

'Dirty bugger, dirty bugger,' she shouts. She was scratching at the window like a wild cat too, and her face was screwed up. 'You dirty bugger. Maybe you like little boys. Or maybe you're mad. I'll get you locked up. I'll get the police. A dirty drunkard. You would drink piss.'

Uncle got up in his shirt tails and went to the window and shot out his fist towards her. He didn't touch the glass. She jerked her head away and spat, then ran for all she was worth. I'm not sure whether she ran because Uncle had shot out his fist at her, or maybe it was because she'd seen Uncle with just his shirt on and it short because he had cut off the front to make a handkerchief.

'If you want to go, you can,' he says to me.

'No, I'd rather stay,' I say.

I was happy when I was with Uncle. He had a good heart and Ma was always trying to get him into trouble. One time she told the police that Uncle was walking the roads at night with a big black coat on, and trying to scare young girls. Uncle never did that. He never did it and he never had a big black coat either. And one time she told the Methodist Minister that Uncle jumped out at her when she was coming home from church. And she said he tore the buttons off her coat and she never had no buttons on it in the first place. The Methodist Minister came to see Uncle about that and Uncle just spat on the ground, as if he had just tasted something sour, and slammed the door in his face.

After Ma ran away, Uncle got up and put on his clothes and so did I. He said you got no peace to sleep around here. He said that folk wouldn't leave you alone. He sat in front of the fire with the bottle beside him.

'I never done nobody no harm,' he says and his lip twitched a bit and I thought he was going to cry.

'I know,' I say, and I was near crying too. But it was the drink with Uncle. One of those big bottles and maybe he would dance or maybe he would cry. I seen him crying before and I cried too. One thing about Uncle, he had a good heart.

He finished the bottle and looked at me.

'You're a good boy,' he says. 'You never done me no harm. Not like some folk.' I didn't know what to say. There was a little tear in the corner of my eye and I didn't want him to see it. I turned and looked towards the window.

'I think it's going to rain,' I say. Then I wiped my eye quick.

'Only you and my mother never done me no harm,' he says.

'Everybody likes you,' I say. He put the bottle up to his lips again but there was nothing in it.

'They tried to get me put away one time,' he says. Then he kind of sobs.

'They tried to get me locked up – but I never harmed nobody.'

'I never seen you harm nobody,' I say.

'I pay for my drink and I ask nobody for nothing,' he says. 'They tried to get the doctor to come and certify me but he didn't come. They said I needed treatment, but it's them that need treatment.'

'They all need treatment,' I say. He looks at me with his big mouth open and there were tears in his eyes. But he laughed.

'You're a funny boy,' he says and he came over and

ruffled my hair. Then he sat down and put his hand on his brow.

'That's right, son. They all need treatment.' His big head shook and he was crying.

'Dear, sweet mother,' he says, 'you are away from it all now. Maybe I wasn't a good son, but I loved you. Dear old mother dead. You went and left me. I loved you, mother, and there's nobody going to say nothing about you.' I sat and looked at him and not knowing what to do. His big soft head and his big soft heart. His shoulders shook. My eyes got wet again, and I went over and put my arm around his neck. He put his arm round my waist and we didn't speak for a long time. Then I say, 'Where's she buried?'

'She's dead, son, she's dead,' he says.

'Maybe we could take her some flowers,' I say. He looks at me. His big red face and them eyes wet and the white of them full of little red lines like a map.

'You're right, son,' he says. Then he stands up.

'We'll get flowers,' he says. He went and put a cap on and wiped his eyes with the back of his hand. Then he took out his handkerchief and wipes his nose. You could see his loose lips moving from side to side.

We started off walking through the fields. There was a fine cool rain coming down. It was nice and cool on the eyes. After we crossed the first field, Uncle put his arm round my shoulder and told me that I would get on, that I had a good brain. He walked fast and my legs were moving twice to every one step of his. I tried to take the same steps as him, because I wanted to be the same as him, but it was hard, and after a while I gave up. Then Uncle started talking about his mother again. He said about how she used to make soda bread and he used to eat it fresh from the griddle with butter on it and the butter melting. And she used to make her own butter too and he drank the buttermilk. It was great stuff. In the evenings him and her sat round the fire and she used to throw potatoes in it to bake. She would sing too. She had a voice that would charm the birds off the trees. It came from her soul. She would sing, 'I cursed and swore at my father, I told him his words were a lie.' It was a sad song, and Uncle sung it to me to let me know what it was like. I could see it all in my mind. I never knew her but I could picture her. She was a fat, cosy woman with grey hair and a dimple on her chin. Uncle was a bit like me, only he still wore the same cap. The big fire and the black potatoes, and Uncle poking them in the fire to see if they were ready. And the house smelling of pipe smoke too. A nice warm, sweet smell. The kitchen was cool and smelt of butter and buttermilk. And sometimes it didn't smell so nice. Sometimes it smelt a bit sour and stale. That was in the morning, just after Uncle got up and the kitchen hadn't started having a nice smell and the big fire was cold.

We came out onto a mucky land and Uncle told me to get onto his back, because it was deep and wet, and I had only a thin pair of shoes with holes in them on. He bumped up and down and his boots sucked in the muck. He was still talking about his mother. He has a little red scar on the back of his neck. He must have been hit with something sharp at one time. His neck went up and down as he walked, like a horse. The lane was narrow and the bushes on either side were almost meeting in the middle, and they were high, too, and wet. But Uncle went straight through them – even the big wet briars that were sticking out. Up near the top there was a honeysuckle and Uncle let go one of my legs and picked a flower. Then when we got to the top he let me down and showed me how to bite the little nipple off the end and suck the honey out.

We walked for a long time before we came to a little new house at the bottom of a good lane. It was built with brick, and it had a thing on the chimney that swayed in the breeze. Uncle explained to me that it was to tell you what way the wind was blowing. I couldn't understand why they wanted to know, and Uncle didn't bother to explain. We didn't walk straight to the house. We went down the lane and into a field, then we went up the side of the ditch towards their back garden. It was full of all sorts of flowers dripping in the fine rain. When we got to the hedge that separated the garden from the field, Uncle signed for me to wait and he bent down and went along the side of the hedge. Then he got down on his hands and knees and disappeared into the hedge. I felt a bit shaky because if folk caught you in their garden they could shoot you. I stood there cold, and shivering every now and then. I stood for a long time. Then I seen the big bunch of flowers coming out the hole first, then Uncle. He had a big grin on his face and he wasn't scared at all. We examined the flowers. They were roses. On the way back Uncle took a long sniff every now and then and he would let me have a good sniff at them too.

The graveyard was grown over. You could hardly see

the graves at all. Me and Uncle went straight to one that had no gravestone. There was just one glass wreath on it, and it was almost covered in nettles. Uncle pulled them out with his bare hands and they didn't seem to sting him. Inside the wreath it said, HERE LIES MY MOTHER, MRS PETERSON, BORN 1876, REMEMBERED BY HER SON ROBERT SOLGER. Uncle wasted no time. He just lifted the glass off and stuck the flowers in and walked away. I thought he might have prayed or something, even though he didn't believe in praying.

We went home and brought the hook and the spade out of the shed and washed them, then we put them back again. Uncle and me sat in front of the fire. It seemed like we had done a good day's work, and we deserved the rest. Uncle was in a good mood again. He didn't talk about his mother anymore. We got the pan out and made mealie crushie. It was easy to make. You just fried the meal. But Uncle said it was good for you. He said there was more in one panful of that than there was in a cow. When it got dark Uncle was almost sleeping in front of the fire. He wakened up quickly and looked at the clock as if he had slept or something. Then he couldn't find his cap and he had been sitting on it all the time. After he found it he slowed down a bit. He sat back on the chair and started waking up slowly. He stretched his legs – tried to pull his face into a pucker with his two hands and then he stretched his arms as if he couldn't stretch them far enough.

'I suppose we better go to the pub,' he says.

Ma never let us alone after that day. She was always scrabbling at the window or thumping the door. She said she would see Uncle in hell. Uncle got more and more fed up. Then one day he goes out into the shed and comes back in with a shotgun.

'What's that for?' I ask him. He didn't answer me for a while, and I asked him again.

'You want to stay here,' he says.

'That's right,' I say.

'Then,' he says, 'if you're going to stay here I need some peace. I need no woman bothering me every day. I can do without that.'

'But you can't shoot her,' I say. He didn't answer, but he looked at me as if he was saying, 'Can I not?' Then he started cleaning the gun. It was a double-barrelled gun and he pulled an oily rag through it and looked down the barrels with one eye closed for about an hour. After it was well cleaned he went into a cupboard and brought out a box of cartridges. He slipped two in the gun and closed it up, then he went to the door and I heard the shot. He came back in with a smile on his face as if he had just shot a lion.

'It works,' he says. Then he took the empty cartridge out and threw it into the fire and started cleaning it again. After he had finished this time he put two cartridges in it and went down and put it at the side of the bed. During the night he wakened up several times to make sure the gun was still there.

First thing he did in the morning was to go out and climb up onto the roof with the gun and sit there. I wanted to go up too, but he told me to stay inside. He sat for two or three hours before Ma came. She had the Reverend

Carson with her. The Reverend Carson was the same thickness the whole way down and his chin and neck were all in one. It was him that shouted at Uncle first. He didn't see the gun at first.

'You give that boy back to his mother,' he shouts.

'You go home or I'll shoot you,' Uncle shouts and picks up the gun and points it at him. Him and Ma walk slower.

'You need to get locked up,' Ma shouts.

'If you don't go home you'll get locked up in a coffin,' Uncle shouts.

'The man above you is watching you,' the Reverend Carson shouts.

'I don't care,' Uncle shouts. 'You just get home unless you want some lead.'

'You'll suffer for this,' Ma shouts. 'You'll go straight to hell. You'll get jail.'

'One more step and I'll shoot,' Uncle shouts. They both stop dead.

'Come down and talk,' the Reverend Carson shouts.

'Maybe you like little boys,' Ma shouts. 'Maybe that's why you never got married or maybe it was because you were too dirty. When did you last wash?'

'You better go home,' Uncle shouts. 'You take one more step and you'll get the lead pumped into you.'

Then Ma says something to the Reverend Carson and the Reverend Carson shouts, 'I studied law, and I'm here on behalf of this woman and I tell you to let that boy go to his rightful mother.'

'Right,' Uncle says. 'If you stay there, then the boy can go if he wants.' Then he shouts to me, 'You can go son, if you want to.' I stayed where I was and there was silence for a long time.

Then Uncle shouts, 'There, did he go?' Ma burst out into a temper and her and the Reverend Carson took two or three steps forward.

'Give him back, you dirty bugger,' she shouts, 'You're a filthy bugger, you'll roast in hell.'

'God will punish you for this,' the Reverend Carson was shouting, 'God will smite you.'

'Stop!' Uncle shouts. But they didn't or maybe they didn't hear him. Then there was a bang and they stopped all right.

'Bugger!' Ma shouts. 'Lazy dirty bugger!'

'You take another step and you'll get it this time,' Uncle shouts.

Ma and the Reverend Carson talked amongst themselves for a bit and Uncle just sat there waiting. Then the Reverend Carson takes two big steps forward and there was a bang. Then he was standing there with an ear missing and Ma was going away quick and the Reverend Carson was going away quick too. I reckon they never thought Uncle would shoot.

It wasn't long before they were out of sight and Uncle came down from the roof and he didn't talk about it. He went and put the gun in the shed and we talked about the land.

OUR HOUSE

Da was reading the paper and picking his teeth with his tongue. Like the rest of us he was doing nothing, and he didn't look as if he wanted to do anything either.

I was lying on the sofa with my eyes closed. Ma was leaning up against the fireplace wondering what to say next or maybe wondering what someone might say to her. Then I opened my eyes and I was right: I had forgotten that I was watching TV.

And that's how it was in our house – not much but we kept alive in case something might happen. We kept the TV on even when it was bad; sometimes I put the sound down and wise people looked worthless or maybe stupid and very funny.

Then my Da put the paper down and Ma looked at him. 'You will set yourself on fire one of these fine days,' he said. But Ma did not move from the front of the fire. She just said, 'Ah well, you'll be free from me then, won't you?' That meant he had to say Yes or No. He picked up the paper and said nothing.

Then I heard Drew coming downstairs. I thought perhaps he might be coming down backwards. He did that sometimes for a change. He went straight over and caught Ma's nose and she wriggled free like an insect, telling Drew to have a titter of wit.

Sometimes Drew would set Da's paper alight at the corner when he was reading it and Da would say, 'For Jesus's sake.' And Raymond and Frances and Peter and me, we would all laugh. Sometimes he would put the wet dishcloth on Ma's face when she was dozing on the chair in front of the fire. Or maybe stick a feather up her nose – then Da would laugh.

We were all not doing much when Raymond and Peter pulled up in the car. Maybe Ma would say something to Raymond when he came in, about not being ever in time for meals. Or maybe she would go on about it being a waste of time sending him to art school and him not doing anything since he left. And him not listening, and her going on and on, and Da saying, 'There's nobody as hard of hearing as those who don't listen.' But nobody told Peter off; he was our brother-in-law and Ma's son-in-law.

'Look, Raymond's got a box,' Drew said, and we were all at the window now except Da.

'I wonder what it is,' Frances said.

'Some damn fool thing,' Da said.

Raymond and Peter were coming up the path, Raymond with his little beard and the big brown box under his arm.

They knew we were looking at them but they didn't look in; they just came up and knocked at the front door.

'Come round the back!' Frances screamed. She had a voice that would cut tin. Da said: 'Don't they know there's a back door.' He always said that.

Frances kept on shouting to come round the back. Drew went and sat down and Ma said, 'They can knock all day, and people watching them.' They kept on knocking on the door. Then Frances went and sat down, and Da got up and opened the door, but they had just gone round the back.

They stopped and ate something from the kitchen table, and Raymond had milk on his beard when he came in. Peter sat on the sofa beside me and Raymond crushed down between us where there was no room for him. Then there was no room for us. The box sat down still in front of him covered with a newspaper. We were all wondering what was in it. Peter looking as if he didn't care or as if he had nothing to do with it. Ma still in front of the fire, wondering if she should scold or not.

Raymond brought home all kinds of things like bottles of spring water, water cress, or anything that's close to Nature. Last week he brought home bluebells and they were unlucky to bring into the house and he brought them in and Ma went mad and hit him with a brush. She knew she was right, and so did he. He put his hand in under the paper so we still couldn't see. Da just left down his paper and looked as if he were working things out. Ma's lips were tight and her eyes wild like an empty TV screen. The rest of us just had our mouths hanging open. Raymond's face looked as if he was looking harder and harder at the sun, then as if he could stand it no more, as if he might cry. His hand still stayed in the box.

Drew was the one who snatched the paper from the top of the box. There lying on its back, was a hawk panting and stiff, maybe wishing it could vanish through the floor, and its big claws sticking into Raymond's hand. There was a little red blood round the skin where the claws had gone in. Drew started to laugh. He laughed when Ma fell out of bed and when Frances fell down the stairs and her feet went through the glass and it cut them.

Da came over and tried to pull the claws out, but as soon as he put his hand near the hawk, its hooked beak stuck in him like an axe. This made Drew laugh more, his eyes closed and his arms stiff and shaking. 'I should have put another shot in the bloody thing,' Peter said.

Raymond looked so angry. Everything had a right to live. When Da set a mouse trap on the landing, he waited till Da got to sleep, then he snapped it off with a comb.

Then I saw Ma, too upset for words, tossing and tossing her hair with her fingers. Da got a pair of leather gloves from the back and pulled the claws away from Raymond's hands. The hawk went mad and grabbed the gloves, and I saw the red bone under its wings where the lead had ripped. It lay on its back looking almost proud, its neck stiff and jerky when the gloves moved near, its eyes like little black brains. It gripped the thick leather glove and clung like a spider, one wing not moving. Then Ma found words. 'Get it out of this house, get rid of it. There is an evil thing about it, get it out I tell you.' Then she pulled a big bunch of hair, and as her feet slapped down on the ground she shouted, 'Get the goddamned thing out of here!'

Then my brother looked at her, his little beard and his eyes just like the hawk. He just said two words slowly: 'Jesus Christ.' He might have been saying it to Ma or to the hawk's wing. Then Ma said it was all Da's fault, that he was worse than Raymond. And Drew said that it had nothing to do with Jesus Christ, that He hadn't shot it. Then Ma realized it was shot on Sunday – you could never have luck killing on Sunday. But she didn't say it because it was Peter who shot it and he wasn't her son and it wasn't dead.

Raymond put on the gloves and went in and brought out a crust of bread. Ma said there were people starving in India and Drew said we could parcel up the crust and send it out. Ma said that we should thank the Lord we had bread and to keep the TV down low on a Sunday.

It did not eat the crust. It just dabbed at it. Raymond talked to it and called it Harry and asked it if it hurt. Drew talked to it too. He said that it was a silly little bastard sitting still in the sky making other little birds dizzy, and had it no sense, hadn't it seen Peter with the gun? Raymond told Drew not to be so silly. Then he put a warm jersey in the bottom of the box and made a kind of bed for it. And Da got some spirits for the gash and Ma went on and on about Da encouraging Raymond, and to get it out of the house before it died. But Raymond said that it had no notion of dying, but that it might die if it didn't eat that day.

Drew got a piece of wood and put it near Harry, and

Harry gripped it, then he lifted it into the air and it fell off. Raymond asked him if he wanted a slap on the mouth. Ma said, the bird was only for starting rows.

Frances got a bandage and Raymond spent hours trying to get the bird's wings strapped in place. He would talk to it and it was hard work trying to get the bandage on when it would not stay still. Da helped him. They were both on their knees on the floor.

When they had finished, Raymond and Da looked round and Ma was still sitting on the sofa. 'I thought you were up in bed,' Da said.

'I'm not going to bed with that thing in the house.'

'Ah sure, it will do no harm; get away up to bed and stop worrying.'

Then the man on the TV reminded us to switch off the set. Nobody spoke. They all looked as if they were arguing without saying anything. Ma looked the same as she did when Raymond was eight or nine and he wouldn't eat his dinner, or even when he was fourteen or more and she left it down in front of him and said, 'You will eat it before it eats you.' Then she would go away and Raymond would throw it out of the window to the hens.

Ma just kept saying – I will sit here all night if I have to – without actually saying anything.

Raymond took the bird out into the shed, and we all went to bed and when we came down in the morning Harry was sitting huddled up towards the dead fire. No one would eat their breakfast until Raymond took it out into the shed. It looked better this morning because its feathers had dried out, but it still wouldn't eat. Raymond walked in and out of the shed all day with cheese and bread, but Harry would not eat.

When Ma had finished washing, she told Raymond to go down to the butcher's and get it some raw meat. He was doing nothing anyway.

He walked to the butcher's and when he got back we were all home from work.

He started to shred the meat, then Drew came in from the shed bending right back and laughing so hard he didn't make a noise. Then he was able to say, 'It ate OK,' handing Raymond the bar of soap with the big gashes in it. Raymond ran out into the shed and we all followed him.

The hawk was lying in the big boiler, the bandage wet with soapy water. Its feathers were wet too, and its mouth was blocked with soapy foam.

Raymond lifted it out of the boiler. He did not need gloves now; its claws were cold and stiff.

Da said: 'Isn't it lucky it took the easy way out?'

Raymond licked his lips and his body seemed to pant, faster and faster, not crying. Not yet anyway. The panting would get louder and he would start running, running through the trees by the river.

We might find him with his arms around a tree, whispering to it.

THE GREEN DOOR

Sam Boyd had a nice big house with a nice big green front door and a big brass door-knocker, and he was able to burn coal in a stove now. But Sam was not liked for many reasons. It all started a long time ago. Sam was never any good as far as I know. I was born when I was no age at all, but I only seemed to come to life since I was five or six, and he might have been good before then, I don't know.

If Sam wants to blame anyone for where he is now he had better blame the Lord, and his wife, because she introduced him to the Lord, and it was his wife's mother and father who introduced her to the Lord. And we all knew the Lord, but the Lord was better to Sam Boyd than he was to us. Maybe we worked for the devil or maybe we worked for the Lord, I don't know, but whoever we did the job for we did it well. That is Pat and Ba and myself. I was Peter. I was called after Saint Peter and Pat was called after Saint Patrick, Ba was called Ba since he was a baby and he was from a big family and he was the youngest, and they had run out of saints.

Anyway the Lord saved Sam, or maybe he was born again and maybe that's why we did not like him. And the Lord said to our families, 'Eat, drink and be merry for tomorrow you may die.' And we could live rough now because he said, 'In my house there are many mansions – come and I will prepare a place for you.' And it was like the new houses in the town, you could only get one if you were poor and had enough money to pay for one. And the Lord said that rich men would not get into the Kingdom of Heaven, so we stood a good chance. And the Lord told Sam, 'Get ye out from among them,' and He told him to work hard now and drink no more and Sam got rich and bought our houses. That was when Da told him that he might not get into heaven now, and Sam said that the Lord worked in a mysterious way – and who was he to question the ways of the Lord, and my Da kicked him in the stomach. When he came round he gave Da a sermon on how to do good to those who hate you, and to turn the other cheek. And he went and took the rent and turned to go in and Da kicked him on his big fat behind. And Sam put up the rents.

When Ma made the tea, Pat and Ba would watch her like a dog would watch you eat. They were not brothers – that is Ba's Da had black hair and Pat had black hair but Pat's Da and Ma had blond hair. But Ma said we had a ginger cat and it had black kittens, and Da said, 'But we didn't know the Tom.' And Ma said that when Ba's Da was out of work for ten years, he went in and sat in front of Pat's Ma's fire and sometimes he whitewashed the bedroom. Then my brother came along with black hair too and we said no more about it. Pat and Ba looked like little mice, and Ba's father wasn't born black, but Ma said he had a bad liver and Da said he worked too long on the coal truck and he looked like a black mouse and we called him Black Magic.

Pat and Ba and me would sit at the side of the big open fire at night listening to Da telling stories, sometimes about Sam or someone else or he sometimes read Robert Burns and sometimes there would be fourteen or fifteen in the little kitchen, and Ma would make tea for them all and I would watch Ba and Pat watching Ma make the tea and Ba licking his nose.

Sometimes it would be very silent when we would get Da to read a letter from someone's son in England and they would be jolly but the old folk might drop a tear and then laugh it off. And then we would talk about Sam till the morning. We all knew we didn't like him, he ploughed the only path we had to the three little houses, he put locks on the gates we had to use and in the winter we had to climb over and pull the bicycle over, and maybe a can of oil or a bag of bread.

It was after my brother James went to the big school in the town that we (Ba, Pat, and me) knew that we could blow Sam's door off. The first two weeks that James was there he learned to make a chair, and we learned to make one. James stole the wood from school, but that wasn't wrong because he said that the Lord helped them that helped themselves. Then one day he came home with paper and powder, and we watched him in the kitchen. Ba saying, 'God, what will it be next?' Then he just watched in a funny silent kind of way, like he had got into a trance. James made liquid then he dipped the paper into it and put it near to the fire to dry. Then, as if it didn't matter, he just touched the blue paper to Ba's fag. Ba was eleven now and he smoked his Da's fags. So did Pat and they were wiser than me now because I couldn't smoke yet. But I was learning. The paper just started to burn; a rim of orange crawled slowly up like the heather in the bog did that dry summer when Ba started to smoke and threw a lighted match away.

When we learned to make that, James brought home some ready-made gunpowder from the school. We packed the gunpowder into a cotton reel and ran some blue paper into it and made it hard with more paper. Then James said, 'Who wants to hold it till I light it?' and I got holding it. It was dark now and we stood in the light of the kitchen window; Pat was smoking as well as James and me and he could inhale now. 'Keep that dog away,' James said, and Pat kicked it, not hard but it went away. I held the thing in my hand and Ba stood at the window thinking, wondering and licking his nose. 'Light the thing,' James said, as if he was the leader, and knew everything. 'Pat, light it.' Pat lit it, and James said, 'Throw it away,' about six times and I watched the blue paper burn nice. Then Ba knocked it out of my hand and I was going to slap him on the mouth but Pat had hold of him and Ba threw it away before he would let us get it, and the dog ran after it like he did when we threw a stick away. When James saw it coming up the yard with the lighted end sticking out of its mouth he said, 'Drop it dog,' then there was a bang, and the old dog gave a painful yelp and died. Ba said it was the best thing we had made yet, and threw the old dog in the river. That same night we made a bigger one for Sam Boyd.

Ba talked about blowing the whole house up, but we said we wanted to blow the door off, and if the house went up too it was bad for him. We only blew some paint off the door the first night, and James made some bigger and better ones, except for two bad ones that didn't go off. We went along there after dark every night, and Ba was the one who pushed it under the door, and we would lie behind the hay shed, smelling the hay and grass and then soon after the bang we could smell the gunpowder as if it had stung our noses. Then Sam would come out and we would curse at him and his big fat belly and sometimes we got so used to it that we didn't even run.

Then one night James told us that he was going to make a real bomb at school the next day, and Ba and Pat and I went into a mad kind of a dream, not saying a lot, just smoking more and kind of happy and frightened. That night we sat in our hideout saying nice things to each other and about James and all our families and me liking the earth and the slimy ferns and the clay on the floor. And we didn't want to leave each other that night, we wanted to stay awake till James came home the next night with the bomb, and I wanted to tell all the people in our house, but I just went to bed and thought I was lying awake. And then it was morning and Ba was shouting in the window, 'Get up to hell,' and the smell of the frying coming in from the yard where Ma was making the breakfast on the oil stove. And me hearing Ba saying to Ma, 'There's work to be done today Mary.' Then I was sitting on the doorstep with my bare feet and Ba and Pat eating bread from my plate and throwing some to the hens. Then it got night quick and James was home, and we followed him into the shed where he opened his schoolbag. It was a long bomb with brown paper round it and written on it was 'The Black Devil.' 'It's made from a half of a bicycle pump,' James said. Then he got out a red pencil and wrote on it, 'To Sam with love from the Lord.' We hid it in the hen-house till it was well dark and we had our supper. 'Where are you boys going,' Ma said. And I said, 'Nowhere,' and Ba and Pat said, 'Nowhere,' and she looked at us with her eyes half closed as if she could read our minds with her eyes half closed.

Ba said, 'We are not going nowhere, honest to God.' And we ran up to Sam Boyd's hay shed.

We got the flat end under the door and lit it, and Pat and I said, 'No need to try no more.' Then Ba started kicking it with his heel and cursing. 'It won't go,' Pat said. Then the door opened and Pat and I ran for our lives, just not thinking but running faster than we could go. We fell into the hide-out just breathing and panting, lying on our bellies. Then Pat and I thought the same thing because we both looked as if we had lost something. 'Ba's not here,' I said. 'He won't ever get caught,' Pat said, looking through the branches just like a mouse. Then we lay there for a long time, Pat lying on his back pulling a fern to pieces and saying nothing. Then as if there was no noise beforehand

Ba pushed through the branches and came in. 'Where did you two go to,' he said and his hands in his pocket and calm and not licking his nose. He sat on a stone and lit a fag and dragged it slow, and speaking like the preacher did after he had bawled his head off for an hour, as if it is up to you brothers. He just spoke slow – 'He came out and his face was red and fat and I looked at him and then I ran too and he ran after me and I was able to look back and he was running like a cow and then he turned and walked back fast and I walked after him, making farting noises at him. Then he went up the steps and looked at the bomb, and then I looked at the bomb, and it was out. Then he hung his head, and I think he was talking to the Lord. And I was ready to run all the time, then I said, 'There's a present from God,' and he looked at me for no time, then he picked it up and I could see that he was still angry, he slammed the door and then I thought this bombing is no good. Then I went round to the side window and I saw him put the rings back on the stove, and Mrs Boyd reading the Bible in the big armchair beside the fire, and him walking quick up and down the room. Just before I was going to yell in the window at him' – then Ba started to talk fast – 'there was a bang like Hell had broke loose and I saw Mrs Boyd sway in the chair. Then I saw the pipe from the stove come down slow and then maybe I went stupid but I saw no more for a while. Then it was all dark, the room was just black and cracking. Then thick black smoke, like rubber burning, came out of the window. Then I thought maybe I'd better go and find yous . . . We got to blow that door off.'

[illegible]

THE LAST WORD

Ma and I were coming up the lane. Ma stopped on top of the hill and spat on the corner of her handkerchief and rubbed my face hard and sore. We travelled this way every morning to school. Then Ma looked up. Flying down the road on her big bike was Aunt Sally, she was the fattest aunt I had. We could see her feet spinning round in quick little circles, her head back and her arms straight, her head flying along the top of the little rows of hedge, then the rest of her body flying and flapping. Ma just stood still and looked, her and Aunt Sally hadn't spoken since the day Ma was going to visit another aunt, and passed Aunt Sally's house without even calling in to say it was a bad day, or even looking in the window, or waving. Then Aunt Sally swerved round into the lane towards us looking at us all the time and pedalling fast. She jumped off and held the bike back like it was a horse, her hair was dyed jet black and her face was covered with pink powder that seemed to fall off her chin. And they said that she had another man living with her as well as Uncle Walter, and she smoked. Maybe that's why Ma didn't call in that day.

'I thought I would come to you first in case you hear it from a stranger.' She was talking fast, and the powder was falling on her black coat, and she was looking at me quick as if I shouldn't be there. She looked at me sad, then spoke to Ma, 'It's his Aunt Mary – she is going out with . . .' 'It's not a Catholic!' Ma yelled horrified. It was as if she had stuck a sword right through Aunt Sally's heart, she howled loud and let the bike drop and stands sobbing. Sobbing like a big baby and covering her face in her hands. 'Pull yourself together,' Ma said and shook her by the shoulders. Ma shook her hard and she was gasping for breath, her shoulders jumping up and down.

Then I don't know why or what happened to me, I just saw the road and the lane and I was sobbing too. 'You shut up or I'll give you something to cry for,' Ma said. That made me worse.

Then it just looked as if I had been crying or dreaming all morning, and I didn't go to school that day. Aunt Sally left her bike at Carson's Farm and we all walked over the fields to our house. Aunt Sally walking as if she might fall on her face any minute and sniffing loud. Ma didn't say anything that would help her, maybe that sniff – sniff – sniff was getting on her nerves, or maybe she still hadn't forgiven Aunt Sally for that day she didn't even look in the window, or say it was a bad day.

When we got home Ma put some coal on the fire, and

made me give my nose a good blow, and I didn't cry any more now. I got under the table and listened.

Ma said, 'If her mother knew she would turn in her grave, and the family all such good Protestants, wouldn't harm a soul.' I lay on my back under the table, Aunt Sally had a little round red mouth that looked as if it was going to suck something, her eyes black like a snowman's eyes unless she was crying. She pulled her dress over her fat knees.

'I say there has been nothing but bad luck since Mary chased that gypsy from the door, and wouldn't give her a penny for the paper flowers. She said, 'Get away from the door you dirty bitch.' And the gypsy said, 'You will never have luck.' And Mary said, 'Shut your face, it's none of your business.' Then the gypsy went out into the lane to the pump shouting, 'Beware of dark men, you will never have luck, someone is going to die.' That was just before her mother died and her only seventy-seven, and now what do you think?'

Ma didn't say she thought anything. Then she told Ma, 'He's got black hair!'

'Well I never!' Ma considered this for a long time, then she asked, 'Are you sure he's a Catholic?' Aunt Sally looked delighted, 'As sure as there's an eye in a goat.' Ma sat back on the chair, 'Well, well! Who would have thought . . . She will have to get out of the house now and who is going to look after her brothers and her father?' 'God knows!' Aunt Sally said, looking into the fire and her head sadly on the side, 'God knows!'

'Will she turn?' Ma asked. Aunt Sally shook her head

slow from side to side. 'God forgive her if she does ... that's all I say.'

Maybe I cried or slept or maybe I was thinking of something else, because in the distance I heard Ma say to Aunt Sally, 'You will have time for a cup of tea,' and then I was up at the chair at the table. Ma put a cup of milky tea in front of me saying, 'I needn't ask you if you want anything or not.' Aunt Sally kept on saying, 'You shouldn't have bothered, sure I'm only after mine.' And Ma saying, 'It's nothing,' and not leaving too much bread on the table – she knew Aunt Sally would eat the decorations off a hearse.

I didn't go to school the next day because the teacher wouldn't believe that I was sick for one day, so it was two months before the teacher sent for me. And Aunt Sally came down to our house every day except for the days Ma and me went to visit her. And I hadn't seen Aunt Mary for a long time except out the window twice when she was coming over the field to our house, and Ma and Aunt Sally saw her and locked the door. I felt sorry for Aunt Mary when she tried the door and Ma and Aunt Sally behind the curtains, and Aunt Mary walking backwards and seeing the smoke coming out of the chimney. I just knew that Aunt Mary was going to marry a black-haired Catholic and that the family were all Orangemen, except Da, and I was too young. But all the rest of her brothers walked with the Holy Bible on the 12th of July and carried swords and got drunk in Catholic pubs.

Then one night when Da came home from work Uncle Walter and Aunt Sally were sitting in the kitchen with their coats on. Da seemed to know what they were there for, he didn't even have time to eat his dinner, he just took off his boots and one pair of socks and rubbed some hair oil into his hair. Then Da and Uncle Walter talked about the weather and the garden, but they didn't talk about anything else. Ma put on her Sunday church coat. When she had first got it, she had no hat so she never went to church: she just talked about it and said she would go if Da bought her a hat. And Da never bought her one. She kept the Lord's day except for hagging a few sticks or killing a hen. We all set off through the fields, Ma and Aunt Sally in front and Da and Uncle Walter and me behind, and getting further and further behind except when Ma and Aunt Sally looked back and then walked fast. When we got to the road, we all wiped our feet on the grass.

Just up the road below Aunt Mary's lane someone had painted in big white letters NO POPE HERE GOD SAVE THE QUEEN. Ma said, 'It must be someone who knows about it.' Uncle Walter said, 'If you believe all you hear you would eat all you see.' And Ma looked at him as if she were sorry he opened his mouth, and he tried to look as if he hadn't said anything at all. Ma and Aunt Sally stood in the lane a bit and Da and Uncle Walter stood out at the road, not looking at each other. Ma said, 'It's your sister, it's got nothing to do with us. Are we going in, or have we come all this way to walk back again?' Uncle Walter went in the lane and Da followed slow and Ma and Aunt Sally watched them pass and then followed. The door was open and we all walked straight through.

The kettle was singing on the stove and the big clock

with its brass pendulum was ticking slow and steady. That's where I made for, beside the big clock. I could stop it or I could give the pendulum a good hard thump and make it tick fast. Grandad sat close to the fire smoking his pipe, his face a little wet with the heat. Grandad seemed to me to have been old a long time. When we were friendly with Aunt Mary I used to like going there with Ma, I would sit on his knee and he would blow smoke into my face, friendly smoke, and I would pull the loose skin on his hands and watch it taking a long time to move into place again. Him and me didn't speak to each other, we didn't have to. Today I don't know whether he saw us or not; he just sat there, too hot and looking as if he had been asleep for years.

Robert didn't look at the others, just keeping an eye on me in case I would stop the clock. I moved away to give him time to forget about me. He picked up the big sandwich he had already taken a bite from and looked at it, turning it over slow and looking at the bottom. Then he lifted the top off and looked inside as if it might be poison, then he put the lid on and took a fast bite and chewed slowly, still turning it in his hand, sometimes scratching his head and looking at it. That's how he ate all the time – he had no trust.

Sandy sat on a stool cleaning a gun, his trousers and boots smelling of dung, his cap too wide for the thin face and the peak of his cap black with stains. His face looked so thin I thought that one eye would do him. Then he let down the gun and picked up a sturdy-looking boot. He spat a brown spit on a cloth and rubbed the toe in little circles.

Ma and Aunt Sally got together on the same stool. We knew Aunt Mary was in because we could hear her in the room. Nobody spoke – Ma and Aunt Sally just eyeing the place out. Then Da said that it was a good day today, better than yesterday and better than the same time last year. Robert and Sandy looked as if they knew what we had come for.

Aunt Mary walked right into the room and stood in front of the fire, facing Sandy – a big red curl hanging over one side of her freckled face.

Da and Uncle Walter went to get up at the same time, then both sat back again and Ma give Da a look and he leant forward. 'I hear you are going to marry a Catholic.' Uncle Walter looked as if Da had taken the words right out of his mouth and Da looked as if he had said what he had come to say.

'If folk got in when they came to visit some folk, and them in, and smoke coming out of the chimney and the curtains moving, then they would hear it from me myself.'

She looked right at Uncle Sandy rubbing his B. Special boots.

'They think they are fighting to go to heaven because if Catholics ruled the country they might not get there. If they go on like this there will be a lot of people get there too soon . . . or maybe not at all.' Sandy stopped cleaning the gun, 'You don't know what you are talking about woman. You should keep that trap closed. What about that bridge the I.R.A. blew up last week? Someone might have been killed.' Aunt Mary looked at the gun again, 'And do you stop someone getting killed with a gun? Is that what guns are for, to keep people from getting killed? Who do you fight for, your country or your people, or for God or the devil, and your people all in your country fighting for the same thing – and one side as silly as the other and they don't know why. Anyway I've got a date and he's not in the I.R.A. or an Orangeman. He was just brought up a Catholic and he doesn't know why, he just likes a drink that's all.' Then she just said the thing Ma and Aunt Sally didn't want to hear but they wouldn't have missed it. That's when they got up to go. Not crying yet. She just said as if to herself, 'I got a baby in there,' she held her belly tight, 'it hasn't read no Bible yet. Maybe it can't read, maybe it doesn't want to read. Maybe it just wants food and affection. Maybe it doesn't know what it wants.' Ma got out of the door first but Aunt Sally was suffering from shock or something, so Uncle Walter helped her out. Da said to Robert, 'I'm looking for a good bike if you know where there's one going cheap.' Then Ma was looking through the door and we all left.

Ma looked at Da and Uncle Walter as soon as we got outside as if they had been bad boys, but she said nothing. On our way back it was Da and Uncle Walter who walked in front. I couldn't hear what Ma and Aunt Sally were talking about. Maybe it was done, whatever we set out to do.

After that the minister came to our house once or twice a week, and Aunt Sally was there too, and Da worked in the garden and I helped him. He was called in twice or three times, then he would come out cursing and digging harder than ever.

Aunt Mary got married quick one day while I was

at school. They didn't tell me about it but I heard them talking when I went to bed. Or maybe it was Ma that did all the talking and Da just saying, 'Give your head peace and get to bed.' One night I got home late from fighting at school and Ma had the big trunk on the floor, and a big bundle of blankets tied up, and a mattress I had never seen before. She put in some cups and plates and knives and forks, and the big Holy Bible wrapped in Da's vest. 'Ma must think she's a giant if she thinks she is going to go far with that load.' Then I saw my trousers and shirt and shoes going in. 'Hey! Hang on Ma, where are we going? And what for? Isn't Da coming too?' 'No, he says he's got to do the garden.'

'I got to do the garden too.'

'No, you're coming with me where you will be cared for and where I can keep an eye on you, your Da can't look after himself let alone you.' That was when Da came in and stood at the door. 'My God Maggie, you are not going through with this.' He looked at me. 'Your Ma is mad, she doesn't know where to draw the line.' Ma looked at him, her back stiff and on her knees. 'You will know where to find me if you want me, but maybe you won't look, maybe you want to stay clear of this. Maybe you don't want to offend your sister, maybe you think that that baby that isn't born yet doesn't mind being a Catholic or maybe you just don't care any more, you just want to stay in the garden.'

We heard the tractor coming and went to the door. Da seemed to think it was funny. The Reverend Tompson was sitting straight upright at the wheel, his eyes behind his glasses looking as if they were sunk to nearly the middle of his head and his nose and cheeks red as if his skin was too thin in places. The cart thudded behind with Aunt Sally sitting flat on her bottom wobbling and the powder falling from her face. The tractor stopped right in front of the door, and the Reverend Tompson switched it off and swung off like a farmer.

'Take it down a bit,' Da said.

'What for?' the Reverend Tompson said.

'Never mind what for,' Da said, 'just take it down a bit.'

Aunt Sally was still sitting in the cart baffled at Da. 'What harm is it doing here?' she said. 'I didn't say it was doing harm, I just said move it down from the front of my door.'

The Reverend Tompson held out his little pink hands as if he were holding a very big ball. 'Look Thomas,' he said, 'it will be handy here, handy to get the things on, it stands to reason.' Da went down and guided him on to the tractor, very strongly, but hardly touching his black coat. He just said, 'Come on man, get it moved down a bit, we want no trouble in this yard do we?' Then he looked him straight in the face, 'And I don't believe in your reasoning anymore, so just take it down a bit and never mind why – it's a free country, so if I say move it, just move it, and never mind why.'

He got on the tractor, Aunt Sally sitting looking over the side like a snowman. He moved it right down the yard a long way as if to say will that please you. Da just picked up the spade that was lying beside the wall and went up into the front garden. Ma shouted after him, 'Give me a hand with this trunk.' But he just started digging. And the

Reverend Tompson and Aunt Sally standing at the place where the tractor was moved from. They went into the house, and the three of them came out with the big trunk, all three of them carrying it right down to the tractor, and the Reverend Tompson trying not to be angry, that was when he was smiling and the back of his neck was red. When we got all the load on and got on ourselves, the Reverend Tompson revved the tractor till you could hardly hear your ears and Da just kept on digging. As we moved through the fields I could still see Da digging and not looking after us. And Aunt Sally wobbling like she had no spine and the tractor bumping, Ma sitting thin and stiff, just looking at the Reverend Tompson's hat and round shoulders, like a beer bottle, her eyes a grey colour just like the tractor and looking as if they had melted a little.

When we got into Aunt Mary's yard, there was another tractor and trailer parked right outside the door. The Reverend Tompson stopped and turned round, his face looking as if it was about to break through the thin skin.

'Look, they've got here first.'

'That's your fault,' Ma said. 'You said you would call for me at a half-past six.'

He turned his head right round just like a corkscrew. 'How could I get here sooner when Mr Carson was away with a cow and Mrs Carson said just take it, but I had to wait till he came back, to ask him to his face for the loan of the tractor, and he said you should have taken it, and it locked up in the shed all the time.'

He drove the tractor right up close to the other one, and a man came out and drove away on the other one without even noticing us and us looking at him. When we got into the house it was exactly the same as before, except Robert wasn't eating and Sandy had taken off his cap and Grandad was sound asleep. The Reverend took everybody's hand in his two little pink ones and shook them up and down like mad. Grandad didn't even know his hand had been shaken. When he shook Sandy's hand he said, 'With the help of these two brave loyal ladies,' looking at Ma and Aunt, 'yes, these two brave ladies, we will help Mary to see the light. We will save the baby before it is born through deep prayer and the Word of the Lord.'

'Looks as if the Catholic priest and her two new relations-in-law are helping her to see another light,' Sandy said, 'and her husband just wants them all to go home and let her be. He says that him and Mary can find the right road for themselves, and maybe when the baby's about ten or eleven it will find the right book to read. Seems to me he just thinks of the bottle and him saying, when the baby's born he will buy a pub and move away out.'

The Reverend Tompson said, 'Look, you and Robert bring in the things, and leave the rest to me and these good women.'

Up in the room two little dark women were sitting on another mattress with a big string of beads and a little brass crucifix lying on another big book. At the end her husband, a small well-dressed man, stood leaning over, his two fists sunk in the blankets. Aunt Mary lay twitching and a little flushed, both arms under the sheets. He looked at all of us and spoke quietly, 'For God sake leave her alone, you are all wasting your time. If this was my house

I would order you all out, but it isn't my house and Mary can't be moved till after – and it won't be long now.' He went over and sat on the bed pulling Mary's head lightly towards him. She gave a little whimper. He said, 'It won't be long now, and I have plans for the three of us.' He bent down and kissed her on the cheek. She smiled or cried a little. He said softly, 'I will be back soon, as soon as I can.'

When he was gone, one of the little dark women, the one with the ball sliding up and down her neck, held the cross up towards Mary. 'He died for you,' she said, 'remember he died for you.' Mary turned her head away, her head looking wet and the red curl sticking to her face. 'I don't care, will you please just go and leave me alone, please?'

Reverend Tompson stood at the door, his hat at the back of his head, and his eyes too far back. He put up his hand and spoke loud. 'I am the way, the truth, and the light, by me if any man enters in he shall be saved . . .' Sandy and Robert burst through the door backwards with the mattress, and he went flying on his face between the two women. Aunt Mary said, 'Can't you please go, all of you, please.'

Down in the kitchen the clock ticked slow and Grandad slept easy. I was pleased just to sit silent with Grandad in front of the fire. I must have fallen asleep. When I woke up Sandy and Robert were talking in whispers. The door was open and I could hear Aunt Sally telling the two women to mind their own business and to get out, but they never came down. I must have slept on and off for a long time, sometimes when I awoke, it sounded as if there was a war upstairs – the Reverend Tompson preaching from the Bible in all directions, and maybe not even looking at it. I tried to stay awake to hear it. There was silence for a long time, I heard the door close, then there was a loud scream like someone had got killed. For a long time I was too frightened to breathe and my body wouldn't move, my heart thumping hard.

The door opened and Aunt Mary's husband came in with Da and Uncle Walter. Da looked straight at me. 'Where's your Ma?' 'She's up in Aunt Mary's bedroom.' Da and Uncle Walter were about to go up when we heard the voices at the top of the stairs. The Reverend Tompson still reading from the Bible by heart. They all came downstairs, Ma with the little dark women with the big ball in her neck, and Aunt Sally linked with the other one.

Aunt Mary's husband went over to one of the dark women and said quick, 'Well, how is she? Mother, how is she?'

She answered in a matter-of-fact kind of way. 'She's fine, but the baby's dead.' She bowed her head and sniffed into a little wet handkerchief.

Then it looked to me as if everyone's eyes were melting and running into one another's.

THE BIG GINGER CAT

Annie lived in a large house, it was so dark and dirty that you couldn't see in the windows. So you can guess what it was like when we heard that Bob had taken a fancy to her, and he came from a nice house where the oilcloth was flowered and polished all the time, and a nice smell of cooking all the time too, not meat.

The only thing I thought was bright about Annie's house was the sea shells. She had three sea shells on each of the five windows, the things we used for ashtrays. I don't know why, because none of them smoked, not her nor her mother. I am sure none of them smoked, not even in secret. We knew everything about everyone around our way. Even when they didn't know we knew, even when we didn't know they knew. Anyway, why should she put them out there on the window-sill for that big ginger cat to knock them down? It was me that wondered that. Then I saw a lot of houses with ashtrays on the windows, but I wondered why she should fall for Bob, or rather why he should fall for her. I could understand him liking the big ginger cat, stroking it every morning he passed, and it rubbing itself up against his legs while he chatted to her. Nobody understood why he should fancy her because she was dirty and lazy and had teeth that stuck out of her mouth, just like a row of those sea shells. They said she stank too, that is if anyone could get near enough to find out. Da said, you didn't need to go near to find that out.

Bob lived with his three sisters, none of them were married although one of them had a daughter. No one knew who had her; she was just there one Monday morning after they hadn't been seen for a while. But that wasn't to be talked about, not even in secret. Bob was forty-one and his sisters were forty-one too. Da said, they were forty-one ever since he remembers.

I went past Annie's big house every day on my way from school, and she came out that old grey door that was black in places where she lay against it, her just looking after me, and me looking back and walking fast. When there was two or three of us coming home from school together, we would wait until we were well past, shout 'China Mouth,' and then run like hell, and her not even chasing us. She would stand in the midden that wasn't a midden anymore; it had grown over with dock leaves and rough grass, shaking her fist at us.

'What do you think of that, him going to marry her,' all the folks around our way were saying.

'Why not,' Da and Ma who lived next door, said. They pretended not to pay any attention to what folks said, letting on that they had lived so long that nothing surprised them anymore.

Ma said to Mrs Carson: 'Of all people to fall in love.' But even Mrs Carson who told everyone that she talked about nobody behind their backs, had to wonder. But she never said what Ma said to Da every night.

Da would say, 'Now who the hell would have the heart to, and anyway she's too old for that.' Mrs Carson never said that; she never said that Annie was too old to have a baby. She said nothing.

I was only ten then, and I wondered what would happen if he took her on. Would she tidy herself up, wash her elbows and get smaller teeth? Would she move in with Bob's sisters, that is if they got on all right, or would he move in with her into that dark big house, and that cat and that wardrobe against the window where the glass was missing, and you couldn't even see in, not even if you shaded your eyes and looked right up close.

And maybe that old woman was sitting in there in the dark, because people around our way had to think hard to find out whether her mother was dead or not. She hadn't been seen for years, not since her husband died. He was found dead one Sunday morning, lying beside a little stream with a wet shirt in his hands, and no shirt on. It was a big funeral. Most people went out of curiosity, because even then you could not see in those windows. Maybe Annie was like her mother, not being able to wash a shirt.

But we had no more trouble thinking hard to find out whether her mother was dead or not, because two weeks before the wedding we got to know what happened. Annie just went in one night seeing Bob, and said straight out, 'Ma, he's going to marry me,' although we all knew long before that. It seems that she just said, 'Well Annie, you won't need me no more,' and died straight away where she was sitting in the old armchair beside the fire. Annie went to bed, and got up early next morning to go and tell Bob.

'What did she go and die for now,' Bob said, 'maybe you want to call the whole thing off.' And her saying, 'No, no, Bob,' and him saying: 'Well, well . . .' and not even asking her in. Then maybe he thought about that big dark house that could be made into a good place, because he said, 'All right Annie, we'll get her buried before the wedding.'

He went over to a tree stump and lit his pipe. She followed him over and stood in front of him, her hands empty and her nylons twisted up her thin legs like a corkscrew, looking at him with those big teeth making her look as if she was grinning at him all the time.

'Well now,' he puffed, 'I suppose she will want to be buried beside your father.'

'No,' Annie said, 'not there.'

'Why not?' Bob said, 'they all seem to get laid down beside their husbands around here.'

'She told me if ever anything happened to her, not to put her down beside him,' Annie said.

Bob stood up and spat. 'She's dead now, she'll go where she's put. The next nearest graveyard is ten miles away.'

'He requested two months after he married her that she should be buried as far away from him as can be,' Annie said, looking at the ground, saliva dripping from her mouth like a dog on a hot day.

Bob sat down for a moment, then he stood up. 'Look, she don't know nothing now, and there's nothing much of him left by now, so instead of spending all that money in dragging her over half of the country, we will put her down there beside him, and none of them will be any the wiser.'

They settled it there and then. He bought a white shirt and took it off just after the funeral to keep it clean for the wedding.

Ma reckoned she never forgave Bob for putting her down beside him, even if it was cheaper.

All the folks went to the funeral. They all took it in turns to carry the coffin. Bob said it was only right to carry it all the way.

It was a very quiet wedding. We watched them go down the road in a special car; no guests, just two witnesses. As soon as they got it over, they both came back to the big dark house. They must just have had time for a cup of tea and a bit of bread when we saw Bob out, digging up the old midden, her standing on the doorstep watching him, her arms folded and looking proud. He dug the whole midden out, and paved the ground with stones, her coming out to the step every day to watch him.

She was still as dirty as before he married her. Ma said, 'If he would take a scrubbing-brush to her, it would answer him better than clearing away that midden.' Then we thought, maybe he would start on her, but he started on the little row of outhouses. He cleaned the dust and dirt out first, then washed all the walls, and she held the ladder until he whitewashed the outside. After about two months, they had four milking cows and two dozen laying hens. They were doing well for themselves. Then one day we saw chairs, wardrobe, bed and the lot sitting out in the yard. Before the day was out, they had cleaned the windows and taken down the curtains that had been there as long as the house itself. Then we could see in. Bob was painting the place from top to bottom. About four o'clock in the afternoon, it started to rain heavily, and the things still sitting out in the yard.

'What the hell's going on here,' Da said, 'I know that furniture is worth nothing, but it will be worth less after this.' 'What in the name of God are they going to sleep on,' said Ma.

About five o'clock it was lashing down worse than ever and Bob was still painting and she was washing the floor after him. The old wardrobe looked clean with the dust washed off it. Ma kept on about the bed getting soaked through. Soon most of the people knew about the furniture sitting out in the yard. We watched out the window at the rain splashing off it.

'It was worth nothing anyway,' Da said, 'but it's worth less now.'

About six o'clock it had stopped raining, and Ma and Mrs Carson thought they would go over and see if there was anything they could do. Da said, 'Never bother your head, they'll never dry that mattress, not in hell.'

They were on their way across the field when all of a sudden they stopped and looked towards the road. We heard the revs get louder and louder. Ma and Mrs Carson standing in the middle of the field as if they had been struck stiff. 'Jumping Jeasus,' Da said, his mouth open and his eyes wider than ever I had seen them. A big lorry had pulled into the yard. On the side was written in big red square letters: REMOVALS. The van went forwards, then shuddered slowly back towards Annie's door. Two men got out and opened the back doors. I thought our house was big before then; then I thought you could put it inside that big lorry. It was as if an invisible string started to pull Ma and Mrs Carson across the field. They just moved towards that lorry, their eyes stuck to it. One of the men went into the house. We could see the doors open, but we could see nothing else. Da screwed his neck and eyes in all directions.

'What do you think is going on,' he said, not taking his eyes from the window.

'I don't know,' Ma said, 'but we'll take a dander over and find out.'

When we got across, there was already six people there, not counting Ma and Mrs Carson; counting them and us there was eleven watching the back of the lorry. All with their eyes and mouths wide open, wider than when the men had to come to that same field to shoot the mad horse.

Bob came out with a sheet of paper and a pencil, and stood at the door. The two men jumped right up into the lorry and pulled the blankets off like they did that every day. We could see furniture like we had never seen before. All a light brown colour, just like fresh wood covered with glass. And that big thick pink mattress. The mattress they had was a khaki colour and stuffed with chaff, like ours.

Annie stood at the door. I got a good close look at her. She was wearing flat heavy brown shoes and a big lump had burst through one of them near the toes. There was red fleshy rims round her nostrils and the eyelashes, and you could see her gums too. She went inside for a moment, and came out with a heavy coat. 'Put this on, Robert,' she said to Bob. 'I'm all right Annie,' he said in a soft voice. Then he looked at her holding it out for him, and he put it on. She looked round at us showing her gums and looking happy. As the men brought the things out of the lorry, Bob put a mark on the piece of paper. Every time they brought something out, Ma took a deep breath and rounded her lips and dunted Mrs Carson who was standing in a kind of trance.

In three weeks' time you wouldn't have known that house. The windows were painted green and you could see in, and no sea shells there any more, and a big black knocker.

He left her to the last. Then one morning early he took her into the town in a milk lorry. They stayed there all day, and when she came back even Da had to admit that she looked a bit better with her new red dress and her hair permed, even if she still had her own teeth.

Bob explained to Da, 'Maybe if she didn't have looks she compensated for them in other ways.'

'What ways?' Da said.

'Well,' Bob said, 'she has to compensate for them with a pleasant personality or a few pounds more than another girl.'

'Yep,' Da agreed, 'and you won't have any trouble with anyone running away with her.'

No, Bob wouldn't have lost her if it hadn't 'a been for that big ginger cat, or if that big cat hadn't had kittens. It all started with the pigs. She bought them. They worked the little farm between them now. It wasn't very big, but that year they had a few crops. We reckoned they were doing well for themselves.

'What's that I smell?' Bob said one night after he came in from the field.

'What are you on about,' she said.

'That smell.'

'Smell?' she said, 'what smell are you on about?' She dumped the champ on to his plate and put a big blob of butter on top of it. Champ was as far as she could think, mashed potatoes and spring onions, that's as far as she could use her mind for cooking.

He left the table and went down the yard following the smell. When he came back, his face was red, looking as if the blood was going to burst his skin. 'Where did you get those pigs from?' he shouted.

She stood at the table as if he wasn't angry, as if he hadn't shouted at her. 'I got them from Sam Macalaster this afternoon, cheap. Why?'

He pushed his dinner across the table. 'Look Annie, I set this little place on its feet,' he said.

'Yes,' she said, 'and with whose money?'

'Never mind that,' he said, 'I set this place on its feet. Am I right or not?'

'Yes, you're right,' she said, 'and those pigs will help to keep it on its feet. In a few months' time those pigs will double their price.'

Bob pushed the dinner further away. His eyes got hard as if they might crack. 'Look Annie, we got cows that give us milk, we got hens that give us eggs.' His voice got louder and almost shrieked away. 'We don't need to kill pigs. We don't need to kill nothing. We got those potatoes to bring us in some money too.'

Annie pushed the dinner towards him and spoke softly, well as soft as she could speak. 'Bob dear, what's the death of a few pigs? One day and it's all over.'

He pushed the dinner away again. 'I will not have it,' he shouted. There was a thin film of sweat over his face now, eyes and all. He wiped his brow and the corners of his eyes. Maybe she thought he was crying. 'Look Annie, we can live all right without killing.'

Then she said, 'All right Bob, I'll get rid of them tomorrow.'

A smile came over his face like a baby's, and his neck did not look as if it was going to burst any more. 'You will?'

'Yes,' Annie said, 'but will you do something for me?' He started to eat his champ and did not pay much more attention to her. 'Yes Annie, I will do anything for you.'

'Good Bob,' she said, 'I knew you would.' Her eyes were not looking straight at him anymore, kind of looking at the back of her mind.

He ate his dinner before he asked her what she wanted him to do for her. She was sitting in front of the fire, her legs coming out in red splotches with the heat.

'What do you want me to do for you, dear?'

'Oh, nothing much,' she said, putting her head back in an offhand, tired kind of way.

'Well, when do you want me to do it, whatever it is?'

'Oh, one of these fine days, if it need be doing.'

'What's it to do with?' he asked.

She pulled her skirt up over her knees in a sleepy way, her face very red too. 'It's to do with that big ginger cat,' she said. Bob had a kind of croak in his voice. 'You don't want to give it away!'

'No, no, it's not that, you couldn't give a cat away around here now.'

It was as if he was frightened to ask the next question. 'You . . . you don't want to do away with it . . .'

'No Bob, no, give your head peace.'

He could see that she was getting a little irritated, and he went and sat beside her. 'I'm sorry Annie, but I think we would be better without those pigs.'

'Yes Bob, you might be right.' She didn't want to say no more.

'I'll stick to my word,' he said, 'I'll do what you want me to do for you.'

Next day Macalaster took the pigs back from her for less money than she had given him the day before. Maybe that's when their marriage started to go to pieces, because she said, 'I will leave you Bob, if you don't stick to your word.'

'I'll stick to my word,' he said, but he wasn't happy. One night he came in and went to put his rubber boots under the stairs where he kept all his old clothes. Then he saw them: five or six little kittens sliding over the top of one another like little furry worms, their eyes closed and the big ginger cat licking them. He did not have time to take off his boots, he was so excited. He ran straight into the kitchen where Annie was sitting in front of the fire again.

'Come here, Annie, come to see this sight for sore eyes!' But she didn't move, she didn't even look round.

'I know,' she said, 'I knew she was going to have them.'

'Well, come and see them,' Bob said. But she didn't look round. She just said in a cold voice: 'Well, when are you going to drown them?'

'Drown them? DROWN THEM . . .' he said. It was as if he wasn't hearing right.

'Yes Bob, drown them. We can't keep all those, and you can't go back on your word.'

'What word,' he said, 'I never said no word about drowning kittens.'

Then she said in a firm voice: 'Bob, if you don't stick to your word, I will leave you.' That night she packed two big bags and said that if the kittens were there in the morning, he would have her no more.

They slept apart that night, and in the morning the kittens were still there. 'Don't go Annie,' he said, and he tried to hold her arm, and she got so angry that she did not go for the bags she had packed, but got a big flour bag and stuffed the kittens into it, them soft and their eyes still closed. She stuck a big stone into the bag and tied the top with a shoe lace. 'I'll do it myself,' she said. He shouted after her, 'Don't go down there and that big flood on!' But she kept going, the bag thumping against the ground.

He held his head with both hands and went into the house and flung himself on the new sofa. Then he came running out and down towards the river after her. Maybe he was thinking of those little kittens leaving the world, and them not even having time to open their eyes. Or maybe he was thinking, if she did it she still might not forgive him. As he got there, he saw her throw the bag into the middle of the brown foaming water. She was standing on the bank about two hundred yards from the weir, on that deep corner.

As she flung the bag, Bob shouted: 'NO, ANNIE!' She kind of looked around, and toppled in more or less backwards. Bob ran as if he was going to jump in after her, but it was too late. The muddy water had sucked her down. She came up twice before reaching the weir, showing her big teeth and seeming to look straight at Bob although it was too late to say anything more. He stood at the edge, beckoning her to come back. She gave a kind of yelp before the brown water tumbled her over the weir, the water weeping down like a big curl, frizzed at the end with brown foam.

Bob stood there in a kind of trance, looking at the water. Towards the middle it was almost still, then he saw them. The bag must have opened and three of the little kittens were swimming from the circle of waves in all different directions. 'Come on, come on!' he shouted. One of them swam towards the far bank and went down a few feet from the edge. 'Oh God,' he said, 'Come on.' Two of them were swimming towards him neck to neck; the sweat was dripping off him as if he was in the race for survival too. He found a large branch, but before he could reach far enough one of them just sank. The last one kept going, gradually getting pulled further down the river by the strong current at the edge. Then he got it. He picked it right out of the water with the stick; it clinging to the stick, he swung it right on to the mud at the side.

His wife was dragged out later about a mile further down the river. Bob said that, had she been that kitten, he could have saved her.

And Da and Ma were standing at the weir, waiting for salmon to go up, and they saw the red thing go over, but they did not know it was her because I reckon they never got used to her in that red dress.

YOU CAN'T BUY IT

We lived in a housing estate. It was the biggest one around. Mrs James lived there too. It was her that her husband left. She lived up at the top end, and was crippled. The Wallace sisters lived next door to her. Miss Wallace was married, so she wasn't Miss Wallace anymore, but they still called her that because that's what she was called before she got married and folk had got used to that name. She was happily married – that is her husband was happy. He lived with both of them and you couldn't tell what was Miss and what was Mrs. They were not crippled but one had her head to one side and the other had her head to a different side. Da said it was because they lived in the middle of a block and one listened to one wall and the other listened to the other wall. They both heard the row the night Mrs James's husband left her. Da said the walls were as thin as arse paper.

'Toilet paper,' Ma says.

'Call it what you like,' Da says.

'You're ignorant,' Ma says, 'God damned ignorant.'

She tried to tell Da about the row but Da said he had enough on his plate. He was watching T.V. He learnt a lot from the T.V. He learnt that water is like netting wire and the world was made out of things like Tadpoles, called Atoms.

'Do you want to hear the latest,' Ma says.

'No,' Da says. 'Give my head peace.'

'Well,' Ma says, 'Jim James ran away with another woman and left Mrs James.'

'What for?' Da says. 'What for? What does he run away with one if he's leaving one for. It doesn't add up.'

'That's not it all,' Ma says.

'You would think he had his fill with one,' Da says.

'She was struck crippled,' Ma says.

'If you remark there's more paralysed women than men,' Da says. 'If you ask me it's laziness. Nothing else.'

'God forgive you,' Ma says. 'Nobody never knows what's in front of them.' She closed her eyes. 'It wouldn't surprise me if there was an earthquake. It wouldn't surprise me if you were struck dead in your sleep and know nothing about it till the morning.'

'Could you not talk about something else,' Da says. 'All I hear about when I come in is about cripples and deaths and things like that. Could you not try smiling.'

'She was struck paralysed with her legs crossed as soon as he ran out the door,' Ma says.

'Laziness,' Da says. 'God damned laziness.'

'If I was struck paralysed I would like to see your face,' Ma says.

'Can you not smile,' Da says. And Ma started smiling all over her face.

'Hasn't it been a lovely day,' she says. 'The flowers in the garden and the sun in the sky.'

Da said nothing – not looking at her. Then she starts singing.

All things bright and beautiful,
All creatures great and small,
All things wise and wonderful,
The Lord God made them all.

'People aren't deaf,' Da says. 'They can hear you through these arse paper walls.'

'They rushed her to hospital,' Ma says. 'The Doctor just came up and took one look at her. He never even touched her. He just said we'll have to take you in to hospital and she said she wanted to die at home. When they got her in they sent for her Next of Kin, and she had put down her husband's name, but he never come.'

She was in there over four weeks. For the first two weeks Mrs and Miss Wallace went in to see her and took her in apples. Then after that they got fed up and nobody asked about her anymore. She wasn't dead or we would have heard about it. But she tried a couple of times. But even then her husband still didn't come to see her. If she had been dead he would have come.

One day the ambulance came up into the estate. Ma was cleaning the windows at the time. She did that when she was on the lookout for somebody to talk to. She saw it stop right outside Mrs James's house and two men jumped out. Ma left the windows and ran up to see if there was anything she could do to help. One of the men told her to open the gate. Mrs Wallace opened the front door. She was a lot thinner than before she went in. One ambulance driver was able to carry her over his arms, her thin legs hanging and still crossed. There was a lot of children hanging around gaping in the door with their mouths open. They were saying she would kill herself again.

'Get away,' Ma says. 'Get away and play.' Two or three of them went away but the rest of them sat on the wire and in the garden. Ma went right into the house and said she wanted to help. The ambulance driver said, would somebody undress her and put her to bed at night. Ma said she would.

When the ambulance went away the children went away too. All the neighbours kept coming up in to ask how she was. Ma and Mrs and Miss Wallace took it in turns to open the door. They said that they thought she would be OK if she had a good rest and the neighbours whispered that you never could be sure of anything in this life. Ma said it was up to God. He worked in an odd way. You could be punished for your grandfather's sins or you could be punished for your children's sins. She wasn't too sure how it worked.

That night Ma and Mrs and Miss Wallace got together and bought three plastic buckets and went round all the houses in the estate collecting money for Mrs James. SPARE A THOUGHT FOR PARALISATION they had written on the buckets. That night they collected over six pounds and two tins of corned beef, because Mrs Malley had no change. The three of them went in together and presented Mrs James with the buckets.

'Put it all into one bucket and bring it over beside me. I'll not have the house clattered up with buckets.' She said that as if it was their job. As if they owed her the money.

Next morning when Ma went up to see what she could do for her she said, 'You can go to the pub and get me a bottle of Gin.' Ma laughed, thinking she was only joking.

But then she said to Ma, 'If you were confined to a chair maybe you would like a bottle of Gin. You might like something to look forward to.' And Ma looked at her sitting with her legs crossed not even able to take one step. If she were deaf and blind as well Ma thought it would be worse. Then she looked at Mrs James's legs again.

'You never know I might be struck paralysed some day,' she says.

'You can thank God you have the use of your limbs,' Mrs James said. 'If I had the use of mine I could go for a drink myself.'

Ma said she would go. She said it was none of her business how she spent the money. She was nothing. She only went from door to door to collect it.

Mrs James said that if she couldn't spend the money how she wanted to, then she might as well not have it. She held up the red bucket and said that they could have it back.

'No,' Ma said, 'I'll get the Gin.'

When Ma went to the pub there were a lot of people there she knew. She told them about Mrs James getting struck paralysed and she wanted a bottle of Gin. 'A bottle of Gin she shall have,' Jim Thompson said and reached Ma a pound. He was drunk on red wine. Ma said she had the money for it but he pressed it into her hand and said he wouldn't speak to her unless she took it.

Mary Ellen behind the bar saw Ma get the money and before Ma knew where she was, she had a free bottle. Ma couldn't make out whether Mary Ellen had given it free to her or whether somebody up at the top of the bar had paid for it. Anyway she never said anything to Mrs James about it.

When Ma got back with it Mrs James told her to go and get a glass. Ma never thought and brought out two glasses.

'I've only got one mouth you know,' Mrs James said. Ma blushed and said she thought her memory was going and Mrs James said would Ma give the windows a bit of a clean, and Ma said that she thought she better go up home early in case Da would come home early and the spuds never on yet.

'All right,' Mrs James said. 'You better go.' But she didn't mean it that way.

Ma said she didn't want to go. It was just that Da would be mad if the spuds were never on.

'I quite understand,' Mrs James said. But she didn't mean that either, and Ma got a cloth and some stuff and started cleaning the windows. All the time Mrs James kept saying, 'You can go when you feel like it.'

Ma was still cleaning the windows when the Welfare man came. He was a little dark-haired man and he smiled at everybody. He came right in and shook hands with Mrs

James. 'How are you,' he said. 'How are you. It's good to see you again.' He had seen her in hospital and had her down on the book except for a few details. He said Ma was a great woman for helping out. Ma said, you never knew when it could happen to anybody, and it was the least she could do. He says wasn't it odd how sick people had more guts than other people and Jesus loved the sick.

'What do you want to put in the book this time,' Mrs James says. And Ma said she better go, and the Welfare worker said that he didn't want her to go on his account. He asked Mrs James if she had any dependants and she said, 'No.'

'That's a pity,' he says. 'You could have claimed for that. Now do you have to pay a helper?' Ma looked at her and then out the window and Mrs James looked at her.

'This woman here helps me,' Mrs James says. 'I give her three pounds a week.'

'Fair enough,' he says, and puts that down in the book. 'I think that's that dealt with.' And closed the book and brought out a folder full of forms and letters and reports.

'Are you getting any support from your husband?' he asks her.

'No, not a fart,' she says. He opened the book again and put that down and then went to the file.

'Is this the first major illness you have had?' he asked her.

'Piles,' she said. 'I got them in that damp house before we moved here.'

'Fine,' he says. 'Now, have you ever had any training of any sort?'

'Never,' she says. 'I only trained how to be a slave to an ignorant man.'

'I think I better go,' Ma says. She had finished the window and a picture of the Queen at the side.

'You stay put,' the welfare worker said. 'I'll not be a minute now.' So Ma started cleaning a picture of King William that was at the other side of the window.

'Have you ever thought of learning Braille?' he says to Mrs James.

'God. What's that when you're at home?' she says.

'It's for people that can't see,' he says. She took off her glasses and breathed on them and rubbed them with her jumper.

'Sure I can see all right,' she says.

'You can,' he says. 'You can now, but will you always be able to see.' He was smiling. 'Answer me that.'

'Well as far as I know,' she says.

'Ah,' he says, smiling as much as to say, I got you. 'Ah, as far as you know, but how far do you know. Did you know your legs would be paralysed.'

'He's right,' Ma says.

'Of course I'm right,' he says. 'Nobody ever knows what's going to happen to them.'

'I agree,' Mrs James says.

'There's nothing worse than to be struck blind,' Ma says. 'I seen one on T.V. And he was smiling.'

'They are brave people,' he says.

'Did you ever see a real one?' Ma asks him. He sat back in the chair smiling. Looking as if he might laugh out loud with joy. 'I have a blind wife,' he says.

'Was she like that when you got her?' Mrs James asked him.

'She was,' he says. Smiling.

'I'd rather be struck deaf,' Ma says.

'It's worse to be struck Mad,' Mrs James says. 'Then you have no sense.' Ma pondered on this for a long time, then she said, 'The world's an odd place, and I'm fifty-two next year and I don't care who knows it.'

'We all die. You can't buy life,' Mrs James says. The welfare worker smiles. 'My wife can read in the dark,' he says.

'Is that the thing I seen them doing with their hands?' Ma says.

'I could never learn that,' Mrs James says. 'That's one thing I never was good at – learning.'

'There's no such thing as can't,' the welfare man says. 'We'll teach you, won't we.' Ma half nodded her head. She didn't know whether to nod it up and down or from side to side. Mrs James had loose skin on her face. She tightened it covering the most perfect set of false teeth you ever saw and let a slow rough fart and the skin went loose on her face again, showing the teeth. Da said it was well seen that God didn't give them to her or there wouldn't be so many Christians in Belfast. He said they were made by the stone mason that made the head stones for the graves at the corner. The welfare man looked down at the files and stroked the hair at the back of his head. She had lost all control over her wind since she went to hospital.

'What about meals on wheels,' he said. Mrs James reached behind the chair and brought out the bottle of Gin that she had hidden when he came in. She was enjoying all the attention. She said to Ma to get two more glasses. 'No not for me,' the welfare worker says.

'It's a present I got when I came out of hospital,' Mrs James says. 'Just a wee drop to wash your throat.'

'OK,' he says. 'Just what you can hardly see in the bottom of a glass.'

They all sat around. Ma had a full glass and he had a nip.

'What's this meals and wheels,' Mrs James asked him. He was a bit tipsy after a couple of sips and couldn't stop smiling.

'She was blind when I got her,' he says. 'And I love her with no eyes.'

'How does she know what you look like?' Ma says.

'She can feel me,' he says, and laughs in little jerks. 'The world is my country, people are my friends,' he says. Mrs James said that that was a good thing to say and Ma agreed. He said he got the saying from a poor man with no shirt and he never forgot it. 'The world is my country, people are my friends.' He said it again.

'Getting back to this meals on wheels lark,' Mrs James says, 'what's it about?' He brought out a little card. On the front was a van that you could see through and there was a nice man in there with a white hat on as long as himself. He was dishing up hot meals. He gave it to Mrs James.

'That explains itself,' he says. 'All you have got to do is put a tick to each meal you want for a week and they come round with it in the van.'

She looks at the other side. 'My God, what's this, Dutch

or something?' She read, 'Chicken Bol-O Vo, Chicken Ro sete.'

'It's just things you know when you get used to it,' he says.

'I'll give it a try,' she says. 'Good,' he says. 'Just put a tick for one each day.'

'Oh here, you do it,' she says. 'Just put a tick at random, I'll see what comes. I'm not hard to please.' He eyed her up and down carefully before he put each tick, as if he could tell by looking at her what she liked. He closed the folder and shook hands with her hard before he left, as if he didn't want to go.

'You look after her,' he says to Ma. Ma said she would.

'My God it was the Fairy God Mother,' Mrs James said when he went out. Ma went and waved to him driving away.

Da was mad when Ma came home. Her and Mrs James had skuffed the bottle of Gin and she was an hour after him. 'When a woman's breath smells of drink and her husband's stomach is empty, you can be sure that man married the wrong woman,' he says.

'It's the first time it happened,' she says.

'It'll not be the last time,' he says. And she started to cry. But he didn't change the expression on his face. As if she wasn't crying. He just got more and more irritated. She cried as long as she could then blew her nose. She made big loud swallowing noises.

'Mrs James is going to get meals on wheels,' she says.

'Jeasus there's more than her needs meals on wheels,' Da says.

But Da was right. It wasn't the last time the dinner wasn't ready. It was every night. Mrs James and her struck up a good relationship or it was more a company – like they had struck oil. Every morning Ma went up there and then down to the pub for a bottle of free Gin. She told Mrs James about that and they split that money and within a week of the welfare man coming she got a book with an order on each page for ten pounds a week that Ma signed and took to the Post Office and she got an order for three pounds a week for looking after Mrs James too. Then after that, five pounds a week came in from her husband – compensation. One night a week Mrs and Miss Wallace and Ma got the buckets and went round collecting for the PARALISATION. Ma and Mrs James split that money and said nothing about it to the Wallaces. Some nights they got twenty pounds between them.

She started learning Braille for a short time, but gave it up because she said that if there was one thing she was no good at – that was learning.

One day Ma and her were drinking and she said to Ma, 'It's all right getting all this money but it's no laugh sitting in here day after day looking at four walls.' Ma looked at the walls and said that she thought it was no laugh either.

'I want you to go and get John Orr the carpenter for me. I have a job for him.' Ma went and told him and he was up the next morning before Ma. He said he had another job to do, but he came to her first because she was paralysed.

'There's the woman there,' she said to him when Ma came in. 'Measure her.'

John Orr took out his rule and measured Ma across the hips and marked it on a piece of paper.

'What's this for,' Ma says.

'A cart,' Mrs James says. John Orr left and said he would put the job in front of all other jobs.

'What cart,' Ma says.

'I'm getting a cart made for you,' she says. 'You can pull me behind you.'

'First I heard about it,' Ma says.

The cart was delivered in three days. There was a strap over Ma's shoulders and one to go round her waist. Ma was happy enough with it but the Wallaces weren't very happy about it.

'Who's going to pull it,' Mrs Wallace asked. 'The woman between the shafts,' Mrs James says.

'You want us when you need us but you don't want us when you need somebody else,' Miss Wallace says and went in and closed the door.

The shape of the seat was just the shape of Mrs James's behind. It just went down in two big hollows.

Ma moved off and Mrs James sat like a lady. They just went round the estate four or five times to try it out that day. One time when they were going round Da was coming home from work. He didn't let on he'd seen them. Going around like eejits and half the kids in the estate running after them. When Ma came home he says, 'Hallo.'

She says, 'Did you get something to eat yet.'

'I did, thank you,' Da says. And he had never said thank you in his life before.

'Do you want a cup of tea,' Ma says.

'No thank you,' Da says. 'And if I want one I can make it myself.'

'Maybe we better go to bed a bit early tonight,' Ma says.

'I don't think there's room in my bed for a donkey,' Da says.

'What are you on about,' Ma says.

'Nothing,' Da says. 'I just say I'm not sleeping with a donkey.'

'How would you like to be crippled,' Ma says. 'Wouldn't you like to get out in the air?'

'I'm saying nothing,' Da says. 'All I'm saying is I'm not living with a donkey anymore.'

'Everybody has a purpose,' Ma says. 'And the purpose God give me is to pull that cart.'

'If it is,' Da says, 'he must have got mixed up and there's a donkey frying a pan somewhere. So I think you better stay up there now.'

'If it's the case of me living down here or staying up there, I'd rather live up there and do my duty that God has given me,' Ma says. So that night she left home.

The next morning early, Ma pulled her all the way into the town and left her with a bucket in front of her at the town clock. She didn't know the town very well but you could see the town clock from anywhere. She went to an office to see if she could claim money from Da, because she was in the right and it was him that told her to get out. The man said she would get compensation all right.

When she came back Mrs James's bucket was full. She took her down an alleyway and they split the money and did a lot of shopping, and then she pulled her out of the town again. There was good money in the town on market days. On other days they went to the horse races or some other function.

After about six months Ma was getting money from Da and they were thinking about buying a little house nearer the town. But Mrs James was getting very fat and heavy and was sick and vomiting sometimes, and Ma was getting thinner.

Ma left her at the clock one day to go and see where the nearest estate agency was. Then she was going to come back and pull her there. She found one and went back towards the clock. On the way she heard a loud scream. She hurried, thinking somebody had robbed Mrs James. But when she got there, she couldn't see her for the crowd standing around. There was another scream and she pushed her way in. Mrs James was lying with her legs open and blood on the cart. Beside her was a newly born baby no bigger than a milk bottle. There was a young girl beside the baby with a basin of water. She must have been a nurse. Mrs James looked at Ma and Ma looked at her. 'And her paralysed!'

'Close your legs,' Ma whispered loud.

'No,' Mrs James said. 'I waited all my life for this baby. He only done it once and it worked. He left me – but it worked.'

'You never said nothing to me,' Ma says.

'Go and tell him it worked,' Mrs James says.

And she closed her legs.

[illegible] another. There was [illegible]
back. On [illegible] went to [illegible] back [illegible]
after the [illegible]

After about [illegible]
Dad and [illegible] land [illegible] another house
[illegible]
[illegible]
[illegible]

[illegible]
[illegible]
back and [illegible]
towards the [illegible]
She [illegible]
[illegible]
[illegible]
[illegible]
[illegible]
[illegible]
[illegible] wiped the paper with a [illegible]
[illegible]
And [illegible]

Other your [illegible]

[illegible] looked [illegible]
He only [illegible]
work.

[illegible]
[illegible]
and she [illegible]

HELL WILL NEVER BE FULL

Da said that hell wouldn't be full till Kate Bradey was in it. She went to bed with her da and had a child. That meant that the child was mad and had bad bones and was her mother's sister and maybe the child's da was her granda. We seen the man going down the railway, but we didn't see Kate Bradey that day. Ma was in the town – and there was nobody to look after us while she was away – because the day before that I hit Mrs Leaves's daughter over the head with a spade. She was my girl friend and I loved her. She said that Da stole her Ma's coal and Da did. So I hit her on the head. Mrs Leaves come and said to Ma that God above would punish me – He didn't – Ma did. She hit me round the legs with a stick for hitting Liz Leaves with the spade. Then when I cried Ma said I done right to hit Liz Leaves and she would never speak again to Mrs Leaves while her arse looked down.

So we had to run wild because Mrs Leaves wouldn't

look after us. Ma heard about the murder when she was in the town. It was round our way that's all she heard. There was seven of us, Jim, John, Jane, Dickie – that was me –, Willie and when Da got a job in the mill store and two more were born she called one Sam-u-el and the youngest Alister Jordan. We called him Al.

It was a child that had been murdered. The murderer had caught the child by the legs and swung its head against a tree. Ma knew that much. It was three miles from the town where we lived. Ma was to get the four o'clock bus, but when she heard the news at five to four she started walking fast and the bus flew past her when she was about half a mile out the road. When she was nearly home old Pat Orr gave her a lift on the back of his dung spreader. When she told him that one of us might be murdered he brought her all the way to the far gate.

She ran across the field and got in with the sweat pouring out of her – and Da's new boots on the dung spreader and the man had just gone down the railway ten minutes ago.

Ma seen that none of us were murdered nor Liz Leaves because she went into Mrs Leaves's house to tell her even though they weren't speaking. When Mrs Leaves heard it she said sometimes she felt like sitting down on her knees and thanking God that we are not dead. Ma said she prayed every night for everybody, and for the children – even if they were dirty. Liz Leaves said she seen the man and he looked like a murderer and we all said he did too. Mrs Leaves said that to be honest she didn't see the man, but she could feel a chill go down her spine about the same time as he went past.

Ma said that we were all to go into the house and stay there. If she caught us out she would give us something that we wouldn't forget for a while.

We seen Willie Trainer coming up the railway. Ma and Mrs Leaves ran across to ask him what he heard. He seen nothing, only Jim Lance – he was sure that it was Jim Lance that jumped over the wire and up Malley's Lane just before he got up to him. We never seen Jim Lance because he spent most of his life in a mental home – he was always mad ever since he was a boy when he stood up on the roof of the house with two ducks wings tied to his arms and jumped and nearly got killed. The reason they put him in the mental home in the first place was because he thought he was King William of Orange and he told folk that the first chance he got he would kill the Pope – he said that the Pope was the devil. Then one night a crowd of men got this bloke to dress up like the Pope and went round to his house to let on he was going to ask him to become a Catholic. The bloke went round – all dressed up and all, and Jim seen him coming and took the shot gun out and shot him on the side of his face and half his ear was blown off too. They got him put away after that. First it was temporary insanity then he got worse next time he got out – he nailed one hand to a cross he made and couldn't get that hand off to nail the other one in – they had to take him to hospital – cross and all.

When Ma and Mrs Leaves come back – they said that it might have been him that did the murder. Willie Trainer heard that it was Kate Bradey's little girl that had been murdered. She was only three. Ma said she wouldn't want to see any child murdered even if it was always going to be stupid and never know anything – like us – and dirty too. The rest of the day Ma and Mrs Leaves and Liz Leaves stayed in our house. Ma said that she would never forgive herself if we got murdered. Liz and I stayed down in the bedroom. I said to Liz if she didn't get up from the bed I would kiss her and she sat on on the bed and put her hands over her mouth and I said I would tickle her. Then I tickled her and she couldn't laugh too loud because Ma would make us stay up in the kitchen. I kissed her and she was giggling a wet giggle – she said she wouldn't marry me – and I put her right over on the bed and got on top of her and held her hands. She whispered if I let her hands go she would feel me under my trousers if I would feel her too. We did – it was nice like a sour itchy feeling and warm. We said we could be like Ma and Da. When we feeled for a long time we said the next day we would build a special hide out just for me and her, and she could take her knickers off and maybe I would take my trousers off too – like we did one day before.

Ned Leaves and Da came home at the same time. They both worked in the same skutch mill – so they always came home together. When they come in we went up into the kitchen.

Ma said, 'What have you two been up to?' and we said, 'Nothing.'

'Can you watch them,' Mrs Leaves said, 'One minute they're fighting the next they're all over each other.'

Ma said if you fell out and stopped speaking every time your children fought you would never speak.

Da and Ned took off their bicycle clips and stood in the middle of the kitchen. They knew all about the murder – it was Kate Bradey's daughter that had been murdered. They had their own ideas about it and they stood there in the middle of the kitchen not letting on to each other what was in their minds – Da said it happened at three and Ned said maybe it did and maybe it didn't, he was saying nothing only he had heard about it before three. Then Da said if his reckoning was right it happened at two. Ned said that Bill Glee that worked in the mill too and lived just across from Kate Bradey's went home for his dinner and seen the child throwing stones at the hens and Kate Bradey was there too watching her over the half door. Ma said that it was an odd world and them sending men to the moon. Da said it was a monkey.

'She must have had a quick death,' Mrs Leaves said. Da pushed his hands hard in his pockets and sniffed loud.

'It was quick and it wasn't,' he said and looked at Ned.

'Is that right?' Mrs Leaves said.

'Whoever it was, and I'm saying nothing – they must have caught her by the feet and swung her head at the tree,' Ned said, 'and she's a heavy child.'

When the big policeman come to the door, Da said, 'Come in, come in.' Ma told us to get off the sofa and let him sit down. He was big and black and smelt like leather. He had a round red face with a slit in it and his chin was sharp too.

Ned said there was no need to ask him what he had come for.

'It's a terrible thing,' he said, 'I have two nippers myself.'

Ma and Mrs Leaves said, 'You don't tell me.'

'I have,' he said, 'two.'

Da said, 'You can't keep your eyes on them all the time or your eyes would never be off them.'

The policeman said that Da never spoke a truer word. Then he said to Da could he have his full name and address – just for the record. Da said his name was Thomas Alexander Kenney. Then he said to Da just for the books, 'Where were you at two-thirty?' 'In the mill,' Da said, 'skutching.' Then he said why to the policeman and he said it was just for the records.

'I want no records on me,' Da said.

'Don't worry, Thomas Alexander,' the policeman said and took everything down in his book.

'Do you know Kate Bradey well?' he asked and Da said, 'Well I do and I don't.'

Da was feeling a bit uneasy because Ma was looking at him but pretending not to. But then he asked her and Mrs Leaves and Ned Leaves the same questions and put the book into his breast pocket and said it was all a matter of formality. But Da still wasn't too happy about going down on the book and he tried to change the subject.

'How do you go about getting a licence for a gun?'

'A gun,' the policeman said.

'I'm going to shoot rats,' Da said.

'You just apply for a permit,' the policeman said.

'Is that right?' Da said. 'Maybe I'll just poison them.'

'Is there many rats around here?' the policeman asked Da in a sneaky way.

'Loads,' Da said, 'They come up out of the river.'

'If you just put some rat poison down, they'll eat it and they go down to the river and when they drink it swells their bellies till they burst,' Ned said. 'I'm telling you I seen them burst.'

'You might be right,' Da said.

'There's no mights about it,' Ned said. I reckon he was fed up with that policeman – asking him them questions too. When the policeman was just about to go Ma asks him if he had heard that Jim Lance was out of hospital.

'Oh he's out all right,' the policeman said, 'But when he was in they ran a bit of electricity through his head so he's calmed down.'

When the policeman went Da and Ned stood up on the floor again. Ned said that them policemen knew their job – Da said maybe they did and maybe they didn't but he wanted to see no innocent man involved. Ma said God was the judge and when the great judgement day came God would hang him. Mrs Leaves said we were all sinners before the eyes of the Lord because Adam ate the apple and Ma said we should all be thankful we are not all killed in our beds at night and men going to the moon.

'It's monkeys,' Da said.

'They shouldn't tamper with them things,' Ma said. She said we should pray for Kate Bradey – not the child – the child was happy in the hands of Jeasus and Kate Bradey was left childless – even if the child was her sister, it was still her daughter. Da and Ned said that before very long they would find out who did it – but they didn't – I found out first too late – sooner than the policeman.

Da and Ned went to work next day but they said they

would have a chat about it at night. Liz Leaves and me were to stay in the house because the murderer, Ma said, might be hanging around. We got out the bedroom window and ran for it. I shouted at Liz that the murderer was behind the big tree eating the roots and she had to stop and wait for me because she was scared. She held my hand then when she got past the tree she ran and left me again. I ran and caught her from behind and put my hands between her legs. Her dress was soft and her skin was sweating. She said if I didn't let her go she wouldn't build a hut with me. I said I just wanted to feel it for a minute. Her breath was like fresh air. She wasn't wearing the blazer that I liked, and I said that while I was feeling her and she said shut up. Then she said we'd better go and I said in a while and she said, 'No now.' She didn't want me to stop it now but she said, 'No' and pulled my hand away and ran. We went up to the side hill, where there was a dig-out. We said all we would have to do would be to put a bed end up along the front and weave ferns and rushes through it because it had been a hide out before and somebody stole the bed end. We could have a coal bag hanging down for a door too. We got a bed end behind Joe Rainey's barn. It took us a good while of the day to get the ferns and the rushes. When we were weaving them through the bed end, Liz said, 'What's that?'

'What's what?' I said. Her arms were all dirty and there was clay on her dress too. She pushed the streak of wild hair away from the front of her face and came closer to me.

'There's somebody in the bushes,' she said, her little heart must have been beating like a bird's – I could feel it.

Then a wisp of grey hair came out of the bushes and a big brown red face. It was Jim Lance, his mouth was open.

'Children, children, children, mad lovely children,' he said. His voice sounded like he was talking through a pipe. He came right over. His teeth were brown and green – and he was shaped like a bow. He held a cigarette between his finger and thumb – the lit end in towards the palm of his hand. He took a long suck – sucking his fingers too and giving sharp little spits. His nails were grooved and brown too. He put one hand on Liz's shoulder and one hand on mine – the hand that was holding the butt.

'Jeasus loves little children – Jeasus loves me – Jeasus loves the world.' He swung his head down like a drunk man. 'And by fuck I love Jeasus.' We just stood there. Liz put her arm round me and held my hand from behind.

'By fuck, I love Jeasus,' he said. 'Do you children?'

'I like him,' I say and Liz says the same. He let us go and sat on the handle of an old plough that was just outside our hide out.

'Good, good,' he says, 'as soon as you two die you're going straight to heaven in a ball of fire – Jeasus you will.'

'You get buried first like Granda,' Liz says.

'Buried my arse hole,' he says. 'Fuck that, you'll go up to the Kingdom of Jeasus in a blaze of glory.'

'Her Granda was buried,' I say.

'Well they done the wrong thing or he was a Catholic,' he said. Then he got up again he put his brown nails up through Liz's hair – it was soft and long but darker than his nails.

'The Lord Jeasus Christ knows every fucking hair in

your head.' He laughed a bit – The inside of his mouth was black. 'By Christ he does. What are you making?'

'A hide out,' Liz says.

'There I step nearer heaven every day,' he says, 'away up to the moon in battleships.'

'It's monkeys Da said,' I say.

'They're all going, monkeys, elephants, cows – like they went before in the big boat – two of everything only snakes and Kate Bradey and the Pope.' He spoke low, 'and maybe rats.'

Liz got some more ferns and started to weave them in the bed end, she wasn't frightened now.

'It's a house fit for a King,' Jim said looking at our hide out, 'Fit for Jeasus himself.' Then he turned round and shouted, 'Fuck off – Go on, fuck off.'

'There's nobody there,' I say but he didn't listen to me. He sat on the plough again and shook his head. Then he got up quick and shouted 'Fuck off' again and there was tears in his eyes. Liz and me went closer to him.

'There's nobody there Jim,' she said and my heart sank.

'It's OK,' I say.

'Son,' he says and he was sobbing very hard and I was nearly crying too. He sobbed for a long time and Liz put her arm round his back. He smelt of tobacco and a dead fire.

'My mother was a good woman,' he said. 'But they buried her – before she had time to go up in a blaze of glory – fuck off,' he said low now.

'They dug her up again,' I said. I don't know why I said that. He sniffed and looked up at me.

'Do you know the truth son,' he said.

'He does,' Liz said, 'They dug her up the next day and Jeasus took her.'

'That's about all I know,' I said. He wiped his eyes with his shiny sleeves and stood up.

'God, I love you,' he said, 'I love the children of Jeasus.' Then he pulled Liz and I tight into him and kissed us hard on the head. Liz giggled. 'I love you – the children of Jeasus,' he said and let us go.

'She's all right now with Jeasus,' Liz said, and he put his fists in the air and walked off up the side hill singing loud – 'For we'll tighten up the rope and we'll hang the fucking Pope.'

'I never knowed he would be like that, close up,' I said.

'If we got a fire going in this hide out we'll make something for him,' she says.

'What?' I say. 'Soup,' she says.

Liz said she would weave the ferns if I got working on getting a stove in. I said it was too far to go back to Joe Rainey's old barn for a tin box for a stove. She hit me on the hand and said, 'Be a good boy.'

I got a box and I got a big stove pipe too to put through the roof.

We worked till after dark and Ma was mad when we went home – she said she would thump some sense into me. She said she would thump the living daylights out of me and she did. When Da come home Ma told him that I might have been murdered.

'There's nothing to worry about now,' Da said. 'They got him.'

'Who?' Ma said.

'Who do you think?' – I knew all along, in the back of my mind.

'Jim Lance,' Ma said and my stomach curdled with sadness.

'Jim Lance,' Da says. 'They should never have let him out in the first place.'

'Imagine,' Ma says. 'Murdering an innocent child – you would wonder what comes over somebody like that to make them do it.'

'Badness,' Da says. 'Just down right badness.'

'There's no hanging now,' Ma says. 'All he'll get is life in jail with good food and a television.'

'Hanging would be too good for a boy like that,' Da says.

'It wasn't him,' I say.

'Don't talk nonsense,' Da says. 'Didn't it take two policemen to take him away – him shouting like a fool that the child was in heaven.'

'Well we'll go up and see Kate Bradey tonight,' Ma says. 'She must be nearly out of her mind.'

Ma took me with her because she didn't want to come back over the fields at night on her own and it dark and her coming from seeing a murdered child.

The child was in a box so I didn't see it and neither did Ma. But Ma wanted to see it – that's what she went for. Kate Bradey didn't seem to want to show her to us. She said 'Let sleeping dogs lie.' She said she wasn't going to open the box now and she would soon call it a day because she had been opening and closing the box all day for folk to look in. Ma said it was a sin before the eyes of the Lord to kill a child. Kate said, 'What's done can't be undone – you can go to the moon but you can't bring a child to life.'

'No,' Ma says, 'Only Jeasus can do that.'

I thought she would have been crying her eyes out and pulling her hair out too. But she wasn't – she was cold and made Ma no tea. She was sitting burning her legs at the fire when we went in – her two thin red knees almost rattled together – and she had her false teeth out. Her husband, or her Da or whatever he was, was sitting on a stool in a dark corner. He said nothing and Kate held the palms of her hands to the fire and looked round at him in an odd way.

You couldn't tell whether she was looking at him because she liked him or maybe she was saying that we shouldn't be there.

When Ma was there for two hours and she didn't make her a cup of tea or give me a biscuit – and them not speaking – then she said, 'We better be on our way.'

Kate said, 'I'm that tired opening and closing that box all day that I can't move.' She sat on at the fire and Ma said that it was OK, she would see herself out.

It was pitch black outside. Ma walked fast – she was always hearing things at night and thought a man was following us down Malley's Lane. But it was a horse.

She told Da when we got in that Kate Bradey was in a terrible state and she thought that this thing would kill her.

Da said, 'Get to bed and don't start worrying at this time of night.'

I could hardly sleep for thinking about Jim Lance, him crying and soft and him not knowing right what he was saying. I thought about Liz Leaves too, her nice warm fresh breath and her liking me too. But in the middle of the night I wakened up and even when I was awake I could still see Jim covered in warm blood and a rope round his neck and his face crying – and I was crying and I had pissed the bed. It was warm – when I put my hands down it was warm like blood. Ma heard me crying and shouted over there was no need to be scared any more they had taken him away. I didn't answer I just cried silent.

When Liz and I went to the hide out the next day – we got the fire going – we said we would make him soup anyway because he might get out of jail. We cut carrots that she said were safe and put them in a tin of water. The fire wasn't very good because the sticks were damp but we thought it would light up in a bit.

We lay on the earth floor looking at it. Her dress was all clay. She was sitting bow-legged and I could see her knickers. They were nice and soft and looked warm over her skin. We had a big bag for a door so nobody could see in but a bit of light came in through the ferns. I sat stride legs over her – she was happy. There was a lot of freckles round her nose and her mouth was juicy. First she put her hands up inside my trouser leg and felt it – then I put my hand under her knickers and felt hers too. After a while she went and pulled the bag to the side to see that there was nobody around then she took off her knickers. I took off my trousers and she sat on her hands and knees and

I got on her. I was warm and nice and sour between my legs and didn't see the face looking in at the side of the bag for a while. When we seen it we let on to be fighting. It was Kate Bradey. 'I seen ye,' she said, 'Filthy.' She was coming right in.

'This is our hide out!' Liz shouts and she was trembling. Kate's face was mad, her eyes were stiff and not looking at me – only looking at Liz – and I don't know what happened and me not shouting and it was happening – and Liz's voice was choking and she was saying my name and Kate Bradey was on top of her pressing her throat. I was mad all my guts were turning mad inside me. Kate's thin legs – blood and nasty bones – holding Liz's legs down and the back of her head almost bald.

Liz's face was bursting with blood and vomit was coming out of her mouth and no noise now and Kate was mad and shaking her head and Liz's head too like a dog killing a rat and I was on top of her pulling her clothes and pulling her thin grey hair – finding no words and biting. A lot of blood was coming out of Liz's mouth – I shouted, 'No fuck fuck ... God shit Christ – my love – you cunt.' Then I was lying there and me with no trousers on and the fire fell down and died like Liz. Her mouth was half open. The blood was on her face with the clay. The bag was away from the opening and I never seen Kate Bradey going. I moved my cold body over beside Liz and put my mouth on to her mouth and on her blood too. I closed my eyes and felt her arm. My throat was sore too and my body was itchy and cold. I wanted just to be like Liz. When the policeman shone the torch on me I held Liz tight. I was frightened – I was frightened of the policeman and Da too. I loved Liz.

'The boy was lucky to get away,' the policeman said. 'She must have gone clean out of her mind.'

My breath was too jerky and deep for me to cry now.

THE GRAVEDIGGER

Uncle Robert lived in a little house but he had a bigger shed. The shed was much bigger than the house. It was made of solid sleepers from the railway, and the house was just made out of thin wood.

Uncle stole the sleepers from the railway. Well, that's not exactly true. He brought them from there. Well, he said, if he hadn't taken them, somebody else would have. One time the Queen was going to come along in a train and, about a year before she was due to come, they got big ambitions to make the track nice and smooth. But either they didn't get down to it or maybe all the sleepers had gone before they had time. Anyway it doesn't matter because she never came. But it did some people good, because them that lived near the railway got their doors and windows painted. At least the Government gave them money for the paint. Uncle tried to get some money to paint his house, but they said he was too far away from the railway. Uncle didn't say much about that. He just said, 'Is she short-sighted?'

The shed overflowed into the house. And Uncle was always trying to get something to put into the shed. He said it was bare looking. He had everything a man could ask for. A woman's bike, a man's bike and lots of parts of bicycles. That was because he used to work at bikes one time but he said there was no money in it. The folk that had money didn't want to part with it, and the folk that hadn't it – well, as Uncle said, you can't take blood from a stone. In the shed there was a horse collar and a cartwheel, although Uncle Robert never owned a horse or a cart. But he did get rich. I reckon it was the new Methodist minister that made him rich. Well, not meaning to.

It was more or less like the Queen. The new minister was to come in January, then he was to come in March. Then he took bad and died. Then there was a new one called the Reverend Glass to come in June. He was young and folk thought they would like him, but he had a row with somebody and never came at all. Then the following January a man like a worm with a black hat on and a pair of glasses came. He was the Reverend Samson. Uncle said they could do without a minister and as far as he was concerned they could do without the church too for it was only causing rows. The thing is, all they wanted to do was preach. All the time there was no minister, there they were, never without a preacher. Every night someone different would get up and shout out how God had saved his soul. I reckon anybody could have got up and done a turn if they felt in the mood. But none of them ever did anything to keep up the church. Half the windows were broken and the slates were coming off the roof and the graveyard was like a jungle. They couldn't get anybody to bury the dead until the Reverend Samson came along. And I reckon there was people there that had been stored away for years before he came. And they all seemed to die when he came too. It was as if they were sitting there waiting for somebody to announce them into the next world. But the Reverend Samson took the bull by the horns. He got a man to put slates on the roof and put in the windows, and he mowed the graveyard himself. Uncle said he would slow down and he did. He drew the line at digging graves.

The Reverend Samson had chased around half the countryside before he came to see Uncle Robert. Uncle Robert and I saw him at the door and Uncle didn't say much. He just said 'Trouble' and didn't open the door. Him and me were cosy and it was wet and cold outside. We sat there with Uncle smelling of Guinness and tobacco. He smelt just like the big friendly man he was. In bed at night I used to sniff him because it made me feel he loved me. He smelt warm. Him sleeping in his vest and him taking big deep breaths, sucking the whole room up, dust and everything. And when he breathed out everything fluttered. His bowels rumbled with Guinness, and his heart thumped on the pillow and the bedclothes went up and down. We had a good close look at the Reverend Samson. He stood there like a big red wet worm and the rain dripped off his hat into the corners of his mouth and eyes, and he took off his glasses and rubbed his eyes till they were almost bleeding with the cold, and then he knocked again and still Uncle Robert didn't let him in. He must have been wet and sore round the collar too because he wiped it round the inside with his finger and made a throwing away motion. Uncle had an odd look on his face. I couldn't make it out. It was as if he was holding a laugh back. I said nothing and thought of the Reverend Samson standing out there in the icy rain. He must have been there for about half an hour and still Uncle didn't open the door. Then Uncle says, 'He's away.' And he let out a big breath that made the fire flicker. Then he sat down and we were cosy again.

But that night in the pub they called Uncle 'the Gravedigger'. Uncle always held his head high and he didn't like being called 'the Gravedigger' anymore than anyone else. And why should he? He was as good as any other man; he bought pints. He said, 'I ask no man to pay for me. I ask no man to buy my drink.' If anybody bought him a pint at closing time and they were staying no longer, Uncle Robert would remember it the next night. And if they didn't come in the next night he would remember it for a week or more, or maybe a year, because for about a year he wouldn't let any man say nothing about that person.

Bob Wilson called him 'the Gravedigger'. Bob Wilson was no good. He was always saying things to Uncle Robert to get him going, or to try and get him going. But it was hard because Uncle never had very much to say to him. He was a little grey-haired man and he had a gold tooth and a neck that looked as if it had been plucked. Every now and then he would pull his mouth to the side and you could see his gold tooth. Folk said he developed the habit since he got the gold tooth and other folk said he was born with it.

'I heard the Reverend Samson came up to see you,' he says to Uncle Robert.

'If you believed everything you heard you just might as well eat everything you see,' Uncle says. He always caught folk out with that one if they had heard something.

Bob Wilson was stuck for words for a bit, then he says, 'What else would he want to see you for?'

Uncle thought for a bit, then says, 'Did anybody say he got in?'

Bob Wilson put his mouth to the side two or three times, then he turned his head away. Uncle took a few big sips and then a kind of grin came over his face. Bob Wilson turns round again. 'It's about time some people worked,' he says. But he didn't look direct at Uncle when he says it. And Uncle didn't look at him when he spoke either. 'Is anybody keeping anybody out of a job?' he says. 'It wouldn't be hard to keep somebody out of a job,' Bob Wilson says. He went up and bought himself half a pint. He didn't have to ask for it. He just put the pint glass on the bar and Birtha filled it up. She brought it back to him, the foam dripping off it.

'Is there going to be a fight over there?' she says. Bob Wilson had tight pockets and it took him a while getting the money out.

'Ah sure the fellow couldn't knock a fly out,' he says, and threw the money on the bar. Birtha says no more, she just gives him his change and kind of gives Uncle the eye.

Uncle loved her. He thinks she would make ten women. She is God's gift to nature. Uncle didn't go in for liking women much. But he knew he was safe enough with Birtha because she was already married. And getting on for closing time he would chat her up. He would say to her, 'Man yer a fine wench. A grand girl.' That was Uncle's idea of chatting women up. When he had said that he always felt he had said enough unless he wanted to stay after closing time and then he would ask her, 'What man could leave your house on a night like this?' And she would say 'I know what you're up to Robert. Well, I suppose you can have one for the road.' But come closing time she would put out the lights and light the old lamp that was dimmer than the one she had and Uncle could sit there till the morning if he wanted to. Then, after that, every time Uncle went up to the bar he would say something nice to her. One night he made a grab at her tits and she blushed. But he had had a fair amount to drink that night.

'There's good money in grave digging,' Bob Wilson says when he sat down.

'Well, I'll tell you,' Uncle says, 'he didn't get in.' Then he sat back and considered the subject closed. He had two more pints before Bob Wilson spoke again.

'You could sign on and dig a few graves in your spare time,' he says. Uncle didn't answer him this time but he seemed to consider what he had said for a long time and next day when the Reverend Samson came round, Uncle let him in. It was raining again and he let him stand in the rain for a bit. He didn't want to seem too eager.

'What do you want?' Uncle asks him.

'Oh,' the Reverend Samson says, 'it's a wet one.' Not paying any attention to Uncle's question.

'If you've come here to save souls you'd better go somewhere else,' Uncle says, and he sat down at the fire and didn't offer him a seat or a cup of tea. The Reverend Samson didn't reply to this either and Uncle says, 'There's plenty of souls to save without saving mine.' The Reverend Samson opened his coat and shook the rain off. Then he scooped the wet out of his collar again and threw it towards the fire. A drop went in. Uncle looked at me and then he looked at the Reverend Samson. 'There's no souls needing saving around here,' he says, and looked back at the fire. Uncle wouldn't have minded his soul being saved but he didn't want to stop drinking. And that's what they all said round our way. First they got their souls saved, then they would give up drinking and go around shouting about it. The Reverend Samson went to sit down then he realised there was no seat behind him and he just stood up.

'I didn't come to save your soul,' he says. 'I came here because I intend to put the house of God in order.' 'House of God, my arse,' Uncle says, and he spat a big tobacco spit into the fire and screwed up his face as if he had swallowed his own vomit. The Reverend Samson was stunned for a minute and then his face went red.

'The house of God is not a place to be mocked,' he says and his face went white again, all except his nose. 'The house of God, my arse,' says Uncle and spat into the fire again. He knew this made the Reverend Samson angry but he didn't care. The Reverend Samson's face went red again.

'You'll not be forgiven for this,' he says.

'Forgiven, my arse,' Uncle says and spits in the fire again. Then he looks at me, looking kind of pleased. The Reverend Samson looked shocked and he went to sit down but there still was no chair there. Then suddenly he got down on his knees and started praying. 'Lord Jesus Christ forgive this man. Listen to my prayers for he knows not what he does. Take him into your heart and save him. Make him an honest man. Give him to me. Give him work and bread. Make him happy. Let me give him a job. Lord Jesus, I know thou art there to hear my prayers.' He had his hands clenched, and his face was facing the ceiling. Uncle looked at me and nodded his head, as much to say, 'What can you do?' or 'He must be out of his mind.' The Reverend Samson went on. 'Take this man into your care. Show him the right road. Make him clean. Thank you, Lord Jesus.' Then he got up and came over and looked at Uncle as if he was expecting a miracle. Uncle looked up at him. 'I feel no different,' he says, 'And I don't expect any man to make me different.' Then he got up and caught the Reverend Samson by the scruff of the neck and led him out into the rain.

'Keep your praying to yourself,' he says and closed the door. The Reverend Samson stood outside for a bit before he went away. I think he expected Uncle to let him in again. I think he didn't expect Uncle to be the way he was.

We had to go to the pub after that. Uncle Robert didn't tell Birtha what had happened. He just says, 'Give me a pint, I need it.' And Birtha says, 'You certainly look as if you need it.' 'Trouble at home,' Uncle says, 'You don't have to go out and look for trouble these days, it comes on its own.' Birtha knew better than to ask Uncle what it was. Because Uncle was a mysterious man and that's the way he wanted to remain. He asked me what I would have and I said only a half. He didn't comment on this but you could tell that he didn't like it. He didn't believe in halves. The first thing he started me off in was pints. He didn't trust people who drank halves. I knew I was letting him down.

'Maybe I'll have a pint,' I say. A grin came over Uncle's face. 'That's the stuff,' he says. 'The stuff will help your blood. It's as good as fresh blood from a bull. It strengthens your arm, it makes your willie grow. It puts iron in your brain and it puts lead in your pencil. It broadens your mind. It puts fight in you. It keeps you out of mischief.' Birtha was standing waiting for the money. She knew that I was far too young to drink, but she paid no attention.

'It keeps the bowels regular and that's important,' Uncle says. Then we took our pints and went to sit at the table beside the fire. Uncle was in a good mood. He took a long drink. Then he closed his eyes as if he could feel it going down. When it had settled in his stomach he opened his eyes. 'This stuff was invented before Christ,' he says, 'B.C. that's what that stands for, before Christ. Well anyway, what does it matter? It's like this business of a.m. and p.m. Nobody knows what it's about. That's what they call time in the Ministry of Labour. I says to the fellow behind the counter, 'What's this p.m. lark?' and he didn't know what to say. 'It means afternoon,' he says. Then why not write afternoon? I'm not stupid, you know. I know what afternoon means, but I can't understand p.m. That sounds like Dutch to me. Anyway, this stuff was invented before Christ. The good shepherds were drinking it one night and they started seeing things. It was a bit thicker then. In them days it was pure blood. They used to drink it first thing in the morning. At that time it came in earthenware jugs. They have some of these big jugs to this good day to prove it. They talk a lot about it in the bible. That's what the Black Sea is full of. Man, I would love to drown there. I want to go there some day just to see what it's like. You can lie there in the sun, you know, and when it gets too hot you just go to the Black Sea and drink your fill.'

Uncle went on and on until Bob Wilson came in. He stopped dead and looked into the fire. There was a bad feeling in the bar. Bob Wilson went over to the counter and shouts, 'I hear they're looking for a qualified grave-digger around here.' Birtha didn't answer. She just got him a drink. Uncle Robert pretended not to hear, and Bob Wilson came and sat on the side of a seat near us. He never seemed to sit tight on a seat. He put his mouth to the side two or three times. You got the feeling from him that he was making faces behind Uncle Robert's back.

'There's good money in grave digging,' he says.

'There's nobody going to pray for a job for me,' Uncle Robert says.

'Oh ho ho,' Bob Wilson says, 'So he got in?'

'He got in and I put him out,' Uncle says. When Bob Wilson came Uncle seemed to get like a big baby for some reason or other.

'I hear you get a good pension when you retire from the grave digging,' Bob Wilson says.

'If some folk would mind their own business,' Uncle Robert says. 'If some folk could use their brains and talk about something interesting.' And he didn't look round at Bob Wilson.

'I think there's nothing as interesting as grave digging,' Bob Wilson says.

Uncle brought out a grey brown handkerchief and wiped the foam off his mouth, then he licked his lips. That's how you could tell when Uncle was upset. If he was happy he didn't wipe his lips, he just licked them.

'I know there's some folk I would like to dig a grave for,' he says, still not looking at Bob Wilson. Then he turned round and looked straight at his gold tooth. 'I would like to see that tooth buried,' he says. 'I would like to see it stop flashing at me.'

Bob Wilson wasn't expecting Uncle to go at him like that. Uncle went up and bought another drink. When he came back he paid no attention to Bob Wilson. He sat and talked to me. He was looking into the fire. 'There's nothing to beat a good fire. There's nothing to beat a good flame. What more does a man want in this world than a pint of the black stuff and big flames going up the chimney? The very first time I had my pint in front of a big open fire, I said to myself: this is what a man lives for.' Bob Wilson was listening. 'You need a wife,' he says.

'No woman to follow, the world is all mine,' Uncle sang to himself. Bob Wilson went up and bought another drink and a packet of potato crisps, then he came back and sat nearer Uncle, where Uncle could hear him eating the crisps. He always ate potato crisps and he knew Uncle didn't like to hear him eating them. He ate very loud, like a horse, and you could hear the wet in his mouth. You could tell by the strain on Uncle's face that he was getting on his nerves. But he didn't say anything. He just kept his back to him. Well, he didn't say anything for a while. I reckon he stuck it as long as he could. Then he turns round to Bob Wilson and says, 'If you would shut that big mouth.' But it just made him munch away worse than ever.

'You're getting high and mighty just because you've got a good job,' he says to Uncle.

'I got no job, 'Uncle says, 'And I don't ask nobody to buy my drink either.'

A lot of people came in and spoke to Uncle and offered to buy him a drink. Some of them offered to buy me a drink too. Still Bob Wilson kept going on at Uncle. Even when somebody told him to lay off. Uncle looked a bit hurt when somebody says to Bob Wilson to lay off, I reckon he didn't like pity either.

Even at closing time Bob Wilson was still going on at Uncle Robert. And he was still munching potato crisps. After Birtha had closed the door, Uncle and me stayed on. We got a bit of peace then. There was a fair amount of people in the bar and they got Uncle to sing songs for them. Uncle could sing anything but mainly he sang songs about women. He always stood up when he was singing. He always stood with his back to the fire. 'How about a song, Robert?' they would all say to him, and he would get up slow and take a long swig from the glass and say that he couldn't sing. Then a pint would be handed to him and he would agree. But he would stand up and drink his own pint down first. Then he would take the fresh pint in his hand and clear his throat and start.

I've got a girl in rawhide
She's everything to me
I've got a girl in rawhide
She buzzes like a bee
She has long toes
And shingly knees
Her legs are very thin
Her cheeks are like a barn door
With the sides driven in

Then he would make sure he had finished that pint before he would sing another song. And he would go to sit down too and everybody would shout, 'Another one, Robert.' His second one would be about a woman that was thrown out of hell because she was so bad. He would put everything into the last verse, and everybody would join in.

For it's true that the women
are worse than the men
When they got down to hell
they threw her out again
With a rifle all, rifle all
Rifle all dill doll doll da day

It must have been about one o'clock in the morning and Uncle was on his tenth song when the knock came on the door. We all moved into the kitchen and stood there holding our breaths. Sometimes somebody would take a swig of their drink and then stand motionless as if they were expecting it to explode. It was a woman at the door.

'I thought you better know, Birtha,' she went on, 'You were the last to see him alive. Well, he won't be back here again. He choked on a potato crisp.' As soon as she said that a loud snigger went out in the kitchen. We all started talking in whispers. But nobody really knew what it was until Birtha came in.

'It's Bob Wilson,' she says, 'He's dead. He choked on a potato crisp.' As soon as she said potato crisp a loud snigger went out again. It was Bob Wilson's sister that came to the door. She had been with him when he choked. She couldn't do anything about it. Uncle called for drinks all round and everybody agreed except a couple of people that didn't know him too well and Birtha. She said she was serving no more drink that night out of respect for the dead. Uncle tried to force her but she wouldn't give in. In the end she let him have a couple of bottles to take away.

I couldn't tell whether Uncle was happy or pleased when we got home. The fire was still burning and we sat silent in front of it. Uncle said nothing, but you could tell his brain was working. After a long time he says to me, 'We must go and see what he's like when he's dead.' Then we went to bed. I had to lie with my arms around him because I didn't like to think about it when people died. But even with my arms around Uncle Robert I still dreamed. I kept seeing this big gold tooth coming out of his mouth.

Next day we went over to his house. His sister had taken it over until after the funeral. She was a thin woman with her hair in a roll all around her head. She had grey hair. She was thin and she walked as if her knees were tied together. She wasn't pleased to see us. It seemed to be more of a nuisance to her.

'We come to see him when he's dead,' Uncle says.

'You better come in,' she says. And walked in front of us and opened the room door. He was in a big coffin, a bit too big for him. He looked much the same as he did when he was alive. He was wearing a black suit and a white shirt and a black tie. On the lapel of his jacket he had a little badge to say that he belonged to the Freemasons. Uncle bent over him and pulled his mouth slightly to one side. He still had the gold tooth. Uncle let his mouth go and looked at me.

'It's a waste,' he says. 'It's a shame they have nobody to bury him.' He pulled his mouth to the side again and had a look at the tooth.

'Maybe you should bury him,' I say. 'You said you would like to bury him.' Uncle pondered on this for a while. Then he says, 'I'll do it.'

We both left. We put down our heads and headed straight for the Reverend Samson.

'I'll dig one grave for you,' Uncle says when he opened the door. The Reverend Samson looked as if he was stripped naked but he wasn't, it was just that he had his collar off.

'There's one to be buried tomorrow,' he says, and he didn't have to say anything else because Uncle just says, 'You mark the place and I'll dig the hole.' Then we left.

Next morning Uncle and me got a couple of spades

and went down to the graveyard. Uncle saw the wooden cross where the grave was to be dug and he looked at nothing else. He just started digging. We dug down until we had a hole about three feet down then Uncle says, 'That'll do him,' and we sat down there until twelve o'clock when we saw the funeral coming in the church gate. While the Reverend Samson was saying the prayer, Uncle just kept on sitting on the gravestone. His eyes were looking far away. Suddenly he got up with a start and started to shovel the clay onto the coffin. Then he realised the Reverend Samson hadn't finished droning on, and he stopped. The Reverend Samson didn't say in so many words, but he implied that Bob Wilson was going straight to hell and there wasn't much he could do about it. They had just walked away from the grave when Uncle threw a couple of spadefuls of dirt on top of the coffin and jumped on it a couple of times, then we left too.

We went straight to the Reverend Samson's house and got the money for digging the grave. Then we went to the pub. Uncle Robert seemed a bit restless and he kept looking out of the window. It got dark and he stopped looking out of the window. He didn't stay after time, and he didn't speak much to people. I couldn't make out whether he was upset because he had buried Bob Wilson or not. But I said nothing to him and he said nothing to me. When we got home he got the hurricane lamp and lit it without speaking. Then he says, 'You stay here. I'm going out.' I felt very lonely on my own when he went out. I had a little cry, then blew my nose and wiped my eyes in case Uncle came back and knew that I had been crying. I thought maybe he had gone and left me.

My heart thumped quick and I almost laughed out loud when I saw him come in. He was grinning. He brought the lamp over to the fire and put his hand in his pocket and brought out his dirty handkerchief. Lying in the middle of it was the gold tooth. He told me to hold out my hand. It felt kind of warm.

'It's warm,' I say.

'Feel the weight of it,' he says. I lifted it up and down. 'It's heavy too,' I say.

'It's heavy all right,' he says. 'It's solid gold. We'll go to the town tomorrow and get it valued.'

That night he put it under his pillow and I dreamt about it again.

MAD PETER

No, I am not making it up. I can see Peter now walking through the fields – that funny walk, whispering to me and tugging at me, and making me bend down and look into the little wren's nest. After the bird flew away, he would let me put my finger into the little hole and I felt the tiny warm eggs, such wonder; the nest was warm too and lined with hair. God, I can't explain it. Later Peter would stand back, his rough bitten nails resting on his hips as if he were King of the animal world, as if he had made this thing himself. I would put my fingers in so frightened, and feel those little soft fleshy babes. Then we sat for days watching the nest, watching the wren flying in and out all the time until one day a little puffy bird hopped out onto a thin branch and swayed a little in the first light of the earth.

We would sit still delighted; the blood in our bodies trickling through our veins as if we had just given birth. Poor Peter who, through the good of civilization, was to spend the rest of his years in a large brick hell where I couldn't even bear to go and see him.

A few years later they took him down our road in a coffin. When they took him away in the first place, they had just put him in a large brick coffin.

After school I used to go over to Peter's shack, him sitting at that table that was only a bit clean at the side where he drank his tea, spinning the big blue mug round and round, and me counting sometimes to fifty.

They called him Mad Peter. Maybe it was because he did what he wanted to do when the mood took him. Like that time last summer when he jumped into the river with no clothes on, and the sun hotter than it had ever been that day. But he wasn't to know Mrs Tompson and Mrs Carson were to come up the side of the river that day. Mrs Tompson and Mrs Carson lived two or three fields away from where we lived and at that time, the only time I saw them was on a Sunday morning marching off to the Gospel Hall. And he wasn't to know that they had made a law in the town, that applied to the country too, that said you could not jump into the river stark naked. And the sun blazed on him and the water was cool and clean.

If Mrs Tompson and Mrs Carson would have gone on past, it would have been all right, but they sat down on the big rock and Peter standing there up to his neck in the water. But they sat there of all places, and brought out cake and lemonade, and him still standing there, fed up, and it too deep to sit down.

Then he shouted, 'Your husbands will soon be home, hungry!'

But they just sat there eating and looking at his head in the water. When he tried to go down, it got deeper, and when he tried to go up, the water got too shallow – so he stood where he was, harming nobody, shouting now and then, 'Can't you get away back down home!' But they paid no attention to him shouting, they just looked at his head in the river.

Then the thing in the river started to bite him, and he shouted louder and louder, 'Get to hell! Get away down home to hell!!' And the thing biting him sore now. They sat there like big lumps of trees. He started to plunge and splash in the river, then he came right out.

They ran, they ran just like women do. He ate the cake and drank the lemonade and lay down to dry, then he fell asleep for no time at all, and when he opened his eyes there was Mrs Carson and Mrs Tompson coming up along the side of the river with a policeman. He pulled the white cloth round him, and ran through the trees and the policeman running too.

Peter ran right through the broken sticks and briars and the policeman running fast and Peter stopping and hiding behind a tree. Then he was out in the open and they both were running fast and the cloth fell around Peter's feet and down he went and the policeman jumped on him. He held Peter down and Peter hit him with his head. I think he was right too – and he could never explain because he could only tell it to me, not saying much and I understood, but I couldn't explain either.

Mrs Tompson brought over his overalls, holding them well away from her as if they might attack her. They kept their eyes closed till he got dressed, and him muttering, 'They won't see anything they never saw before.'

They took him to the town. I think that was the first time he was in the town. He was bound over to keep the peace for one year or he would get jail, and after that year if he jumped into the river with no clothes on, he would get jail too. But Peter never broke the peace. Not as far as I know, not even when he shot the Pope. Maybe that was my fault. Anyway the Pope he shot, was dead a long time ago. It was the day we borrowed the shot gun to shoot the TRESPASSERS PROSECUTED sign that they had put up beside the railway.

In the dump near Mrs Tompson's house lay the Pope – the frame coming to bits anyway. None of us knew it was the Pope, not even Peter, so I bet Peter a fag that the couldn't blow his head off. He went right up close and shot a hole right through the picture. I only gave him half a fag because he went up too close – that is, he had to give me half a fag because he was teaching me to smoke and he had promised me a fag before then. Mrs Thomson came out. She said that that was blasphemy and Peter gave her a big smile. But she didn't tell the police, not that time anyway.

It was very odd the way it happened because after that Mrs Tompson and Mrs Carson got a problem, a kind of problem that Peter wasn't bothered about at first. Because he didn't think about it, but they did. It was all about Peter not wearing a suit on Sundays. They went on and on about it. Sometimes Peter stayed out in the fields for hours and hours. It all happened so suddenly. One Sunday I called over to see Peter, and he didn't come to the door, so I went in. He was sitting at the table with a little card in front of him that said, 'Knock and it shall be opened,' and a new looking suit on him.

'You can't come up the plantation in that thing,' I said. He just sat looking at the card, him in those big padded shoulders.

'I don't get it,' he said, not looking up.

'You can't go up the tree in that black suit – what you going to do? Just tell me and I might just go up there on my own.'

'I don't get this,' he said. He turned the card over. The back was blank.

'What you going to do? Just sit and look at that card or help me go and get that magpie,' I said. He handed the card to me.

'Do you get that?' he asked.

'Yep, you knock somebody's door and they open it. Come on, get that suit off and – where did you get that card from anyway?'

'A man.'

'What man?'

'He works for Jesus.'

'Look, I will only ask you once more: are you coming or will I have to go up there myself and get that young magpie, and tame it myself too.'

Peter stood up. His big wide shoulders and him only thin underneath, and those trousers that first belonged to Mrs Tompson's husband, and she cleaned them and pressed them and cut a bit off the legs.

Later on in the day when we had got the bird and put

it into a big box with some bread crumbs and a big wide wire front so that it could see a lot and get plenty of air, Mrs Tompson and Mrs Carson came round the back of Peter's shack. I didn't look at them, but I guessed they were both standing there with Bibles in their hands. 'It is up to you, Mr Price.' And that was the first time I knew Peter's surname. 'You know now what the Lord says: Follow me.' They talked for a long time, and it sounded as if they were going somewhere good and Peter wanted to come and if he was wise he would go – they couldn't force him to come but if he didn't it would be his own fault.

On the Monday the man from the town who worked for Jesus came twice, and on the Sunday I saw Peter going to church with Mrs Tompson and Mrs Carson. They all had Bibles. Mrs Carson was walking in front and looking back at Peter, and Mrs Tompson was walking behind. She had him covered as well. For the first two or three Sundays Peter came home early, and Mrs Tompson and Mrs Carson stayed behind to eat the body of Christ and drink his blood. One day Peter stayed behind too. He told me about it afterwards. He got a piece of bread and a little glass of wine.

It was about a month later when Peter had got his first job. He had to dust the seats of the Gospel Hall and turn on the heat and fill about forty or fifty glasses of wine, ready for the end of the meeting. They gave him ten bob which he put into the collection plate before he handed it down the pews, and which he took back after, as well as a few shillings extra. But I wouldn't have come there that day, only when I went to feed the magpie in the morning, it wasn't there. I thought Peter should know as soon as possible. So I went to the Gospel Hall and found him filling up a big tray of glasses with red wine. The hall was cold and hard and empty and wooden and shiny. Peter was in the little back room and that was a bit warmer but you still got that empty feeling. And you had to talk in whispers. Maybe because it was Sunday or maybe because it was a Gospel Hall.

'It's not there,' I said.

'What's not there?' Said Peter.

'The bird.'

'Who said that?'

'I went to feed it this morning and the box was empty,' I said.

'You sure?'

'Yep.'

He handed me a glass of wine. 'Do you believe in Christ?'

'Yep.' I downed that glass and Peter downed one too, and another, and another; as he handed them to me, I downed them.

'Any holes in the wire?' he asked.

'The wire is full of holes; it is netting wire.'

He grinned and kept handing me the glasses, and started drinking out of the bottle himself.

'I reckon Mrs Tompson stole that magpie,' I said. We smoked a fag between us and I started to feel a little dizzy. 'I do, I reckon Mrs Tompson stole that bird.' I stuttered. Peter smoked the fag until it burned his fingers before he threw it in the bin.

'You think she took it then?'

'Yep. I do. I know she did – I think.'

We finished all the glasses and another bottle and I think I must have fallen asleep. I just remember the smoke blocking my throat. I was being lifted and carried, and then I could breathe again. Peter was shaking me and saying: 'You OK? You OK?', and the water was running from his eyes and his face was dirty looking and he had no eye lashes anymore.

'You OK, my boy?'

'Yep.'

I was lying in the little field beside the Gospel Hall. The flames in the Hall were cracking and the smoke covered all around.

We went back to the shack and Peter changed into his old overalls again because most of his suit was burned away.

The man who worked for Jesus came twice that afternoon, and the next day he came with the policeman. I sat at the back of the shack and I heard them saying, 'Where did that suit go to, and where did you go to on Sunday morning?' And Peter just saying, 'Can't you leave me be. I didn't go anywhere, anytime.'

The next day the big car come driving right across the field, right up to Peter's shack. There were three men in it: The man who worked for Jesus, the policeman and another man with a little beard and rat-coloured eyes. Mrs Carson and Mrs Tompson came half running across the field. The policeman and the man with the little grey beard walked right into Peter's home as if he knew him well.

After about half an hour he came out with his little white hand on Peter's shoulder. 'We are here to help you,' he was saying to Peter.

Peter did not look at me but I could see that he had been crying. My stomach was crying too, but not my eyes.

JUSTICE

In Ireland that day the sky was just a big bubble of hot blue air. And if anyone had been looking through it they would have seen me lying outside a garage on a little slope. The garage was red, white and blue and so was the shop beside it. I was lying there every day for five weeks – just thinking or maybe not even knowing I was thinking. The sun was as hot that day as it was one summer when I was a child. James lay beside me with his Wellington boots and a big red woolly sweater right up round his neck. Yellow curls hung over his head wet and dark. Bill sat up resting his back on his hands. He was brown – chest and all, and he wore no shirt. His hair was too short – even to catch. James said he was that colour with working in the garage and not washing. But he said he was out in the sun every day that summer.

We lay there, not bored or if we were we did not know it. I opened my eyes. The girl in the shop had cleaned out all the dead flies and bees, and had stacked two big pointed stacks of cornflake boxes at each side of the window. I tried to think what she might put in the middle but I couldn't think. I never could think for myself not even since I was born.

I never made up my own mind to be a Protestant, but I was one right from the beginning or before. And Da was an Orange Man – Ma said he was right to be that, because William of Orange fought for us in 1616. And he fought for us and God and freedom. That word freedom made me excited but I got confused between God, King William, the Pope, Jesus and Hitler. It seemed that these people were all after the same thing, but I wasn't sure what it was. For a long time I believed that Jesus got burnt in a fire in Ireland when I was five. Then I went to Sunday school and they told me that Jesus died 1,900 years ago. I knew I was not all that old. Then I went into another class, there they told me that Jesus was alive today and he died 1,900 years ago to save my sins and I wasn't even thinking about being born then. Hitler got burnt in that big fire that I went to the town with Ma to see, and a big barrel fell from the fire and burnt Ma's leg. Catholics believed in God too, but they were wrong – that was the Pope's fault, him and King William had a fight in the Battle of the Boyne – King William won, God was on his side. It was all fights – God and the Devil made heaven and earth, then they had a row and God pushed him out of heaven and he fell to hell.

Maybe Da was wrong that time when him and Mat next door made that shed between them. Da wanted to keep the key, and Mat wanted to keep it too. Mat kept coal in the shed and he said Da stole it, so in the end Mat built his own shed. Jesus and Peter fell out too and I reckon Jesus and God fell out as well, because when Jesus was on the cross, God wouldn't speak to him – and he said 'My God, My God, why has thou forsaken me?' God never answered, that is if He was alive. He might have died because the man at Sunday School said that God was the same as man. That might have been right because when I was six or seven and my little brother who was three took sick for three months, I prayed to Jesus for a long time then prayed directly to God, before he died. But Ma said that it was God's will and Da said he was too good to live. I must have been wrong because they were fighting for God and country all my life where I lived.

When I looked the girl in the shop had put a big cardboard ice cream in the middle of the window. She brought a chair and a magazine out into the sun – looking hard at the magazine but maybe thinking about us. She was a nice girl with fair wavy hair falling onto the pages. Sometimes a farmer would come down for petrol or oil and help himself or maybe wait a long time until Bill decided to get it for him. The sun shone hard and the whole village was in a trance, the sky filled with blue air.

Far in the distance a plane throbbed and moaned too far away to see. The man who sat stiff at the porthole had not fastened his seat belt. He was carrying news about his son. He had spent three weeks in London without a cap on, the cap that stayed on his head even on Saturday nights when he rolled in the ditch and cursed the Pope.

He had stayed in a hotel near the hospital where his son had the heart operation – sometimes lying awake all night listening, listening hard in case he heard his son crying. But he heard nothing but the noise of traffic outside the hotel. The hotel was an expensive one, at least to Joe Miller it was, but it did not cost him a penny, nor did his flight.

James stuck one leg up into the air. His trousers were covered with dried pig dung.

'How long can you keep your leg up?' he said.

I put my leg up, and Bill lay back and put his up too. James started to count. Bill had a long leg, his boot was dull black with oil. We held our legs up for a long time. Then the girl from the shop shouted, 'What's wrong, are you lot going off your heads?'

'Shut your mouth,' Bill shouted back.

James started to laugh into himself, and let his leg fall with a dull thud on the ground. Bill swung his big leg over and knocked mine down. James twisted his boot. They wrestled and rolled down the slope, Bill making snorting noises like a pig. James sniggered loud and grabbed Bill between the legs.

'Oh for Christ's sake let go!' Bill shouted. Bill broke loose and made a grab for the girl. She ran, he caught her dress.

'I'll shout my head off if you don't let me go,' she shouted.

He was big and strong, he held her arms down and ran his big dirty hands up under her dress. There was a loud shriek of brakes and a lorry pulled up on the road.

'Let me go,' she shouted, 'there's somebody coming.'

He let her go, and as soon as he turned she kicked him on the behind and ran into the shop, her arms up like a fairy.

The man in the lorry was young, he bowed his head over the steering wheel for a while before he got out. His face was a pale, weary-looking colour and his eyes were a smoky grey. He wore a pair of jeans and an open-necked shirt. He walked without bending his legs, his neck looked as wide as his head. The lorry was green and was carrying boxes of apples. They sold a lot of fruit in the shop. Joe Miller bought two or three pounds of apples on his way home from the pub on a Saturday night, as well as half a pound of boiled sweets to suck in church on Sunday morning.

We lay on the slope again. I could see under the new-looking lorry, a little oil dripped from the bottom like sweat. The young man lay over the counter of the shop talking to the girl for a while. He straightened himself up and came out and took four apples from the box that was open. He gave us one each and took one into the shop. Bill munched the apple with his strong white teeth, his eyes darting like little devils all over the place, he munched core and all. James turned onto his stomach and threw his core at the wheel of the lorry. That's when he saw it.

'Mick Kelly and Son, that's a right rebel name,' he said. We all turned onto our stomachs, Mick Kelly and Son was printed on the bottom of the lorry door.

*

Old Joe had been up in the sky for some time now, he knew that if he put his hand into his pocket and brought out his watch it would not put the plane off balance, but he didn't do it all the same, nor would he eat the salad in front of him. There were two knives and he might use the wrong one. If they gave him back his case that would be good enough. They put it into a bus before he got into the plane and he'd never seen it since. All that was in it was a few of his own things and a towel and a pair of pyjamas belonging to his son. He would be glad to get into Kelly's car at the airport, Catholic or no Catholic. Kelly had helped him a lot and he was still curious why he had paid for the trip for him. He was new to Joe's district and he knew nothing about him except that he was Catholic and he knew that even before he came, and even the name would have told him that. Joe's wife said her prayers had been answered that night when Kelly left the house, not even waiting for a cup of tea.

Kelly came to the door and asked Joe if he could have a word with him. Joe was surprised to see him. Really they were enemies, they had been born on opposite sides of the fence, but Kelly had a look about him, a kind of softness in his eyes, so Joe said, 'Sure, come in.' Kelly came in, but he never took his coat off, he never even sat down.

'It's your son,' Kelly said, 'I hear that they are going to operate on him.'

'Yes,' Joe said, 'I signed the paper, you see he is not twenty-one yet. He told me to sign it himself, you see, what could I do?' Joe was so used to holding in his feelings now that his body felt stiff as if it was held together with long pieces of iron. He remembered his son lying in the local hospital, both hands lying outside the bed wet and white, his face thin and too tired to cry anymore. He just said to his father, 'Sign those papers, Dad,' and turned his head to the side, not to see his father's face. Joe had stopped kissing his son when he was about six but when he saw him lying there that day – limp and soft-looking, he felt like picking him up and holding him close to his body.

Kelly pressed him on the shoulder. 'You did the right thing Mr Miller, take my word for it.'

Joe felt a little delighted twist in his body, no one had said that to him before.

'Sit yourself down, and take off your coat,' Joe pleaded. But Kelly stood his ground, he was a stubborn man in many ways. 'Where's the boy going to have the operation?' he asked.

'In London,' Joe said, nodding his head slowly from side to side, and not looking at Kelly. 'They tell me they can work miracles there nowadays.'

'Yes,' Kelly agreed, 'It's true.'

'We can ring up every day,' Joe said, 'And see how he is. You see he has no friends over there. It's a Godsend, the National Health flies him over, pays for the lot.' He smiled. 'We will send him books, he is a terrible lad for them books.'

Kelly was a big man compared to Joe. He shook him by the shoulders. 'You're going over there Mr Miller,' he said.

Joe felt a little bit frightened, but he tried to look brave. 'What do you mean? I can't go over there,' he said.

'Why not?' Kelly asked, his eyes were firm and fixed on

Joe. The only time Joe had come across a thing like this was when someone wanted to fight. He looked to his wife maybe for help, but she paid no attention to him.

She just said slow and soft, 'It would be a comfort if he could be with him, Mr Kelly.'

Joe kind of straightened himself up the best he could. 'You're a stranger Mr Kelly but I will tell you the truth, we can't do it on our money, we thought about it enough. You see ...'

'That's OK,' Kelly said, 'I don't expect you to go to London and stay in a hotel on your earnings Mr Miller.'

Joe said nothing, he didn't know what to say, he didn't know what Kelly was on about. Kelly eyed Joe for a while, slowly putting his hand into his inside pocket and bringing out a clean-looking brown envelope, he reached it to Joe. Inside was a plane ticket and a lot of pound notes.

'Oh no, Oh Jeasus no, I can't take that,' Joe was muttering to himself, and looking at it as if it was a miracle.

Kelly looked at the clock. 'Well I must mosey along. If that flight doesn't suit, you can get it changed, and if you call over with the wife in the morning she will arrange the hotel for you.'

He was gone and Joe still talking to him. 'Why? Why? God Almighty, why?' When he looked at his wife she was smiling, but there was a tear running down her cheek.

On their way to the airport, Kelly stopped at the garage for some petrol. Bill, like the rest of the people in the village, wondered how Joe got the money to go to London, and them that knew Kelly just thought that Joe had got a lift with him as far as the town, because they said that

Joe was one of the loyalest Orange Men that ever walked on two feet.

'But I can't understand why you should do this to someone you hardly know,' Joe said in the car. He didn't mention religion.

'I might tell you when I come to collect you,' Kelly said, keeping his eyes on the road and smiling to himself.

The aeroplane fell a little, and the Captain said something through the speakers. He could have said that they were going to make a crash landing for all he knew. People around him started to fasten their seat belts.

When James mentioned the name Kelly I got excited, when a name like that was mentioned you thought there was going to be a war or something, you had to curse the Pope, stick up a Union Jack, or beat hell out of a big Lam-bam drum or something. Last week in the village there was the opening of a new Orange Hall, the second in the village. There was a turnout of about twenty bands, and when I saw the Orange Men walk behind with their Bibles and swords, my stomach thumped like my heart had fallen into it. This was war – real war and freedom. The very next night the IRA blew up a bridge five miles away. We talked about it all the next day in the village, saying what we would do. There might be a civil war in Ireland, saying it would be terrible having to fight for our country. And we were excited, as excited as ever we were, in the back of our minds saying: Let there be war, let us fight for freedom, let us fight, let us fight for God, let our fathers and brothers get killed – then that tiny bit of our minds saying: Let us . . . not fight too much.

That night the Orange Hall was opened. There was no war, but there was a big fight outside the pub where I was standing waiting for my father to come out. A man crashed through the crowd with his bicycle, a little Union Jack sticking up from the handlebars, and he had a bottle sticking out of each pocket. 'To hell with King William,' he shouted, and him only joking. Suddenly he, bicycle and all were lying on the street. A big man smelling of drink and Brylcreem was standing with his fists closed, two men trying to hold him back. The man on the street just lifted his head slow, trying to smile, when the big man kicked him right in the stomach, and a child started to cry, and the crowd moved in. The police moved in with their batons flying. For about an hour there was nothing but women and children crying and men shouting. I was shaking all over because I was excited and nervous, and very frightened because I had lost my brother and father. It stopped when three men were taken to the police station with the blood running out of them. I found my brother later, he had been in with the crowd and only got a cut lip.

The girl came out to the shop door and shouted to Bill, 'Will we get a box of these apples?'

'No, sure to hell the last ones we got went bad on us,' Bill shouted back. The young man came out behind her. 'You never got apples from me before. You tasted those, they'll keep for ages.'

'Are you new on this job?' Bill asked.

'Yes,' he said, 'I'm just trying to build up a trade around this way.'

'That's a right good name you've got,' James shouted and winked at me.

The young man came over and sat down beside us. There were little blue veins running down his white arms, and branching over his honey hands. Bill offered round his cigarettes. He had a heart of gold, people said, but no sense. Young Kelly did not take one, he said that he had to give them up.

'Are our cigarettes not good enough for you?' James asked. 'No,' he said, 'I can't afford them for one thing.'

James did not have to worry about money. About two years ago he found out that the people who had brought him up were not his real mother and father. When he found out he did not get angry, he just made them suffer, he made them pay out for everything, he said that they owed that much to him for not telling him who his real parents were.

Bill lit the cigarette, then put the match close to young Kelly's face. Kelly moved his head backwards and Bill followed him with the lighted match. Then when it was about to burn the point of his nose Kelly blew it out.

'You blew out my match,' Bill said, in a serious voice, the way you would talk to a child.

Kelly tried to be friendly all the time. He laughed, still trying to be friendly, 'Is that your car down there?' he asked, 'It's a fine looking model.'

'Just keep your eyes off that car,' Bill says, 'I don't trust you boys.'

Kelly laughed again, then he eyed the car carefully. 'No but seriously, I like it.'

'Take your eyes off the car,' I said.

'You heard what he said,' James said.

I had no idea that we would do what we were going to do, and I hardly remember how it started.

When old Joe got out of the aeroplane he was a little unsteady and amazed to find that when he yawned he could hear a lot more than he thought. He followed the rest of the passengers into a big glass building. It was hard to believe that he was back in Ireland, but Kelly's warm handshake confirmed it.

'Come on, Mr Miller,' he said, 'Get your case, and let's get into the car, and hear all about your son.'

'What's your first name?' James asked Kelly.

'Mick,' he says, 'Like my father's, they call me young Mick.' He had his hands locked over his knees and he rocked back and forth. Although it seemed as if he wouldn't sell any apples he still stayed. Bill threw gravel stones, hitting Kelly's head.

'Stop throwing those stones, James,' Bill said, pretending that it was James that was hitting Kelly.

Kelly said nothing, not even getting angry. He got up and went over to the lorry and kicked the spare.

'Could you put a drop of air in this wheel for me?' he asked Bill. 'Sure,' Bill said, 'Anything for a friend.'

James sniggered and we all went into the garage. In the garage it was cool and dark. Kelly got the air-pipe and sat on his knees blowing up the tyre. He was just about to get up when Bill tightened his big greasy arms round him from behind. Kelly did nothing, he didn't even try to get away. He laughed, and Bill shook him, then he lifted him up onto his feet and pushed him over towards James. He almost fell up against James. James spun him around and pushed him towards me. He staggered across the floor. I am using all my strength to push him to Bill again. I don't know why I do it, I reckon I just want to be like them, I wanted to be on their side. They are men, they can drink and argue and go with women, and spit like men.

'Ah, ah, that's enough, boys,' he pleaded as he staggered over to James trying to hold himself back. James gave him a hard push to me again. His head was down, but I could see that he was still trying to smile. He got my arms and clung onto them for a moment like a drunk man.

'Use your strength, use your strength!' Bill shouted.

I tried to push him away but he held on. I had to try hard, because Bill and James said that I was strong for my age. He held onto me tight, but not hurting me. Bill came over and plucked his hands off me and swung him to the floor.

'I'm sorry,' he said, as his shoulder struck the floor.

'Did he hurt you?' Bill asked, lifting my arm. I could have said no as easily as saying yes, but I said yes all the same.

James kicked him on the feet. 'You see, you hurt the young fellow.'

'Sorry, lad,' Kelly said to me. He tried to get up, I held my arm. He made for the door. Bill and James stood guarding the door, every time he tried to get out they pushed him back. His shirt was torn and dirty at one side.

'Please, boys, I must go. Please,' he pleaded.

'No, no,' James said, 'Stay a while, the fun's good.'

Kelly stood still for a moment, breathing quick and shallow, then he made a break for it, but they both caught him, and he gave in straightaway without any fight.

'Come on, you rebel, where's the fight in you?' Bill asked.

But he just lay between them, his eyes misty and his eyelids glazed white. They dragged him to the back of the garage.

'Come on, sport, where's the fight in you, you must be older than any of us?' James said.

He did not say anything, he just straightened himself up, as if he had been asleep for a minute or two.

'I think we'll have to try him,' Bill said.

'Yes,' James agreed, 'What's he guilty of?'

'Of blowing up a bridge,' I said. I must have been thinking about that bridge a lot since last week when it was blown up.

They pushed Kelly into the corner and we all stood in front of him. Bill picked up a hammer and thumped the bench. 'Silence in the court!' he shouted. He looked at me. 'Will you ask the prisoner the questions?' I felt a funny feeling come over me, a feeling that everyone was on my side. They must be like this in a real court, I thought.

'What's your name?' I asked Kelly. He was smiling, I reckon he thought we were joking. 'What's your name?' I said again, in a firm voice.

'Michael Kelly,' he said.

'And your age?'

'Twenty-eight,' he replied.

James put a black wooden wedge in front of him. 'Take this Bible in your hand and read the words on the card,' I said.

'I swear by Almighty God to tell the truth, the whole truth, and nothing but the truth, so help me God.'

Then we were serious, we were all serious, even Kelly himself.

'Where were you on the 25th of July last at midnight?' I asked.

'In bed,' he replied.

'In bed,' I said, 'How do you know you were in bed at that time?'

'I looked at my watch.'

'But you are not wearing a watch,' I said.

'I lost it,' he said.

I looked around. 'Do you expect us to believe that?'

He went to go out of the corner but Bill pushed him back.

'Let me go,' he said, 'Please let me go, I want to go home.'

James got a strong piece of string and held it up to me. 'The prisoner shall be handcuffed, Your Honour,' he said.

Bill held his hands together and James tied them. Then Bill went into the office and brought out a thick red car rug, and wrapped it around me. 'You must look the part,' he said.

The robe was warm, the sun was white and dusty through the small window. I don't know what happened, crowds of people started to move in and out of my mind, swords, Bibles and banners pitched in my brain. I started to talk fast.

'Where were you on that night?' He said nothing. 'Did you blow up that bridge? You are guilty, you are guilty, you are doomed, you will suffer like Christ, like Hitler, you will suffer in the name of the Lord, you are guilty.'

'Here, here!' I heard Bill and James shouting.

My face glowed. 'You are unclean, you are mixed up, stupid, you have got a will but you will not use it, you should have thought for yourself, like God and the Devil, not listening to others, but going your own way!' I was shouting now. 'We shall have to fight for freedom, for God and freedom, the whole country shall be free, we shall praise the Lord, we shall think you are an example of mankind's stupidity, and you shall suffer.'

I thought I was dreaming and I tried to wake myself up. Then I saw him in front of me, Bill pushing him back, his shirt up over his trousers. 'You shall . . .' the words were cold and strong, 'You shall hang by the neck until death, and may God have mercy on your soul.' I tried to bring myself to, I was real, but had I just been dreaming?

'Here, here,' James and Bill were shouting and Kelly had still got his hands tied.

'All right, all right,' he said, 'The joke's over, can I go home now?'

James went to the boot of an old car and brought out a thick rope.

'Give it to me,' Bill said.

He made a loop and placed the rope around Kelly's

neck, and threw the rest of it over a beam. I held the end of the rope, it was thick and hairy. Kelly did not try to laugh any more now, his eyes were very moist and his lips were pale.

'Please, boys, stop now, please, I can take no more, I want to go home.' He licked his lips all the time.

Bill placed a big box in front of him. 'Go on, stand up there.'

Kelly tried to hold back and Bill pushed him, him trying to hold back, maybe trying to hold back from crying now too. Maybe if he cried we would let him go. Bill and James both pushed him, me standing with the thick rope in my hands.

'If I go onto that box will you let me go?' he asked.

'You never know,' I said, 'We might.' He got on the box and I held the rope tight.

Then I saw Bill take a swing with those big dull black boots, and Kelly's mouth open. He kicked the box right up the garage floor. Kelly fell and the rope slipped right out of my hands. His shirt was under his arms. A big pink curved scar ran up the side of his ribs, with a little row of pink dots where he must have been stitched. His mouth was still open and his breath short and shallow.

'You shouldn't have kicked that box, Bill,' I said. My mind was clear now, no God nor Christ nor Hitler nor King William nor Pope or Devil, but there was Michael Kelly.

'I'll ring the doctor,' James said to Bill, 'You'll know not to go so far next time.'

*

Old Joe sat in Mr Kelly's car, they were coming into the village, both of them were happy.

'So it was a success,' Kelly was saying. 'So when will he be coming home?'

'Ah, not for a week or two,' Joe said, 'But that boy of mine is as happy as a king with those nurses making a fuss of him, and a pile of books beside him.'

Joe did not laugh aloud, he was too old to show those strong feelings now. He held his face straight going through the village.

When they came up towards the garage Kelly elbowed Joe.

'Look, there's my lad's lorry there, he had his operation eighteen months ago now and he's as fit as a fiddle. He has a helper to keep him from lifting too much but he did not come today, but Mick would not stay in, he said he would go out and do a bit for himself.'

'My boy's the same,' Joe said. 'He wants to be independent.'

JENNINGS TALKS TO . . . IAN COCHRANE

(Interview by Paul Magrath, Jennings Magazine, 1985)

Ian Cochrane was born in 1941 in Antrim, Northern Ireland, and played truant from a variety of jobs before becoming a full-time writer. He had his first stories published in Faber & Faber's *Introduction 4* (1971) and *Penguin Modern Stories* (1972). Since then he has had six novels published: *A Streak of Madness* (1973), *Gone in the Head* (1974), *Jesus on a Stick* (1975), *Ladybird in a Loony-bin* (1977), *F for Ferg* (1980) and *The Slipstream* (1983).

He is a short, stocky, sandy-haired man, with a roving eye and a mischievous sense of humour. We meet in his favourite pub and loosen up over three bitters before returning to his Bayswater flat for a 'lunch' consisting of four pints of Guinness and a packet of salami. His small and not particularly tidy kitchen is dominated by a large, potted avocado tree, the spreading branches of which have been decorated with little plastic flowers. 'I grew that from a stone, it's twelve years old,' he says, looking for some clean glasses. We settle by the gas fire in his living room which, with an old wooden desk by the window and a white painted filing cabinet, is also his study. 'Will that thing work?' he asks, as I produce my microcassette. I assure him it will, and we each open a Guinness.

Do you like being interviewed?

Yes I do. I enjoy being interviewed. I don't know why it is. I think it's sort of getting attention. I'm sure everybody wants attention in some way or other, no matter whether they're going to break a glass, write a book or whatever.

Do you think a writer has any obligation to explain himself beyond what is stated in his work?

That's difficult because ... (*sips Guinness*) I was thinking about that. Not really to explain himself. But if I could tell people really how I feel about writing, I would. I think I could attempt to tell you that, when you ask the next question.

What am I supposed to ask now?

I think there's an attitude that life is secret, and secret to the individual person, but I don't think that's true. The difference between me as a milkman and me as a writer is that people would want to know me as a writer. If I could explain that difference then I would like to. People tend to think you know something that they don't know. I don't think you do. Some writers maybe do, who've studied philosophy etcetera. Most of them have the same feelings as everyone else. They're trying to discover what it's all about. I feel that . . . really the writer is able to sit at the typewriter and explain his different feelings and emotions. If you sit down and feel in a particular mood, you could just stay in that mood; but if you allow the moods to move then you can probably write easier. Well, you probably do. You have to. You have to let the moods move between anger, violence, love, passion, softness . . . observing the sort of things in your mind that you've observed earlier in order to make the story move. You could keep just to one particular mood and it could be an angry mood or it could be a love mood, and you could maybe write a poem about winter or about someone you loved and that's two minutes. But if you're writing a novel you've got to allow your moods to change. I think that's a problem. When I used to teach I used to find people had that problem.

Are you saying the range of feelings which a writer can feel is greater than the range which any one of his readers can feel?

I'm not too sure whether it's greater. People don't like to admit to feelings they have. I mean if I told you now, I feel like doing something drastic or if I said I'm bored, I don't want to talk, you'd probably take that as a little bit offensive, but if I was writing a book I'd be able to say that I'm bored or I feel like going for a walk or whatever. You feel freer in your thoughts. I could throw a chair out the window or something, but I can't do that in normal life so easily.

What drove you to write?

Er . . . (*pauses to light cigarette*) I'm not too sure. I think I come from a society that I didn't feel was right. I think that I was born into a world that I expected to be different from what I found it. I wanted more feelings, more emotion, and I could understand it in other writers. Disappointment, I think; the feeling that the world could be different. I don't really mean change the world. I mean express angry feelings, bad feelings, good feelings, love feelings. I'm sure before you're born, you've got feelings and you expect the world to accept those feelings.

You were brought up in Antrim, Northern Ireland. What was that like?

We lived in a little house right out in the country. The house wasn't even as big as this flat, so there were seven of us sleeping in one bedroom, about the size of this room. I'm not too sure whether that affected me at all or not. It probably did, in a way, because of the relationship between my parents. But I don't think I realised we were living in poverty. We felt quite close, as children.

You describe, in several of your early novels, moving into a new council house. Did that happen?

Yes, we did. I think that was a bigger move than I thought at the time. We had been living right out in the country and I always got the idea from my mother that the other children – the children in the village – were better than us. They always wore uniforms to school. I continued to go to the old school, which was a real little two-roomed country school. There was a teacher at one end and what they called the 'master', a man, at the other end. At about seven or eight years old, you'd move into the master's end.

So it's much as described in *A Streak of Madness*?

That's right. The teacher in that book is based on a teacher I had in this little country school. He wrote a couple of books himself.

Did he encourage you to write?

Yes, he did. I was very bad at spelling, very bad at grammar and what have you. I didn't like school. He's probably what people would regard as a progressive teacher, and he was a very good teacher. I wrote little articles about home life and the people around, and he liked those.

How much of your material do you think is autobiographical?

When people talk about something being autobiographical, do they mean as opposed to something that doesn't exist or hasn't taken place, or what? It's not science fiction, it's in the real world that I'm living in. It isn't my real life, it isn't just autobiographical. But I draw from my own experience. I don't place my novels in India or anywhere I've never known or never had any experience of.

Do you see writing as a means of escape?

Yes. I think I did want to escape from my environment. I'm not too sure. But I think that part of the reason for writing was that I found that I could do it without much effort. Laziness maybe. I don't really like getting up in the morning, I don't really like going to bed at night; I feel as if sometimes there is energy going through me, almost like a voice in my head. When I'm working hard on something, I feel the typewriter can't go fast enough, with all the feelings and the dialogue going through me. I don't think 'I'll write about that' and then set it out and write about it. It just comes to me.

Do you write directly onto the typewriter?

Sometimes I do, mainly I do now, because my writing isn't so good. It's very difficult for someone else to retype it.

So you don't, for example, make your own notes first and then type from those?

I've tried that several times. Going out into the park or sitting in a cafe and taking notes. It doesn't really work. No, I think probably I just take notes in my head. I feed myself.

Do you rewrite or change your work later?

No. Not really at all. I might do that a bit more with this next book I'm working on because it seemed as though I was moralizing or getting things right and wrong – and I think it's wrong for a writer to get that feeling – and it doesn't work. I haven't shown it to my editor yet, it's something I felt reading it back myself.

Are you very critical of your own work?

I'm critical for my own benefit. I feel that editors are quite good. In my experience, if they point out something that's not very well written, not very well explained, so far I've tended to agree with them. They understand your own work and they don't want to change it drastically. There's no great conflict.

Have any authors particularly influenced your writing?

Yes. William Faulkner, I would say, definitely . . . and Albert Camus. I'm not sure if you can say that it's an influence in the sense that you can follow them. I think it's more saying: 'I can be better.' That's very pompous I know. I think Faulkner is a very good writer. He leaves a lot unsaid. People often think space, the gap between two things, doesn't really matter, but it does matter. And Camus – I think I first read *The Outsider* – I liked him partly because of his calm couldn't-care-less attitude; and him being accused of it, people expecting him to have feelings. But there are other writers, who have a great deal of feeling.

Are there Irish writers who've inspired or encouraged you?

The one that would obviously come to hand is Joyce. I wouldn't feel so strongly about *Ulysses*, though he's got that stream of consciousness and so forth. I'm not too sure whether that's original. *The Dubliners*, the short stories, I thought was much better. A lot of feeling. But I'm not too sure about the unconscious business. I mean, what's the unconscious? I'm not too sure. I've never understood *Finnegans Wake*. Maybe I ought to go back to that soon. I don't know.

Why bother?

Well, I have been writing a piece – and this'll be part of the next novel – about a baby before it's born, during its being born and shortly afterwards. I find it very moving, very confusing to think about, and I've been trying to find a sort of language to do that, to describe that. It's very difficult because you don't have a way to do that, to describe how it is, sitting in a pram or whatever, and everything keeps changing around you continuously, a bit of silver paper in the wind, or a tree, everything moving like great pulses – it's very difficult to put it into a language. I want to do it in a language that could be understood but yet would be the child before it's born. When I was writing about it, I think I rediscovered about being a baby.

It sounds ambitious.

Well, this is only part of the book. The book is really about the person only having so long to live. But I'm only doing it like that because if he's only got so long to live, he can feel anything he wants to feel and he can do anything he wants to do. I mean, financially, he can't really; but he can say anything and he can feel what he wants to do. I'm only about a third of the way through the book, and I'm not too sure how it'll end.

Reading your books, I get the impression that they are not very carefully planned or structured beforehand. Are they?

I do make a structure . . . a bit like an underground map, or like a river flowing. But I change course, I change my mind. I've started off thinking that I knew the end but I've never been able to. I allow the writing to move its own way. I couldn't write a well-constructed book. I don't want to. You could listen to some radio programme, one of those plays or something, and you know the ending as soon as they've begun. I don't like that. Most people seem to start with a big finish and then work back from that. I would rather go along and enjoy the atmosphere and the dialogue, and I'm not heading for the end when I start at the beginning.

Your dialogue is particularly good. Do you collect examples, make notes?

If there is anything about a person who naturally feels that they can play an instrument or paint a picture or that they have a voice in their head, then I would say that's the gift I have. I don't do anything towards that. I don't even try to listen to people's dialogue. It comes into my head without any effort. Mostly when I'm not sitting at my typewriter, unfortunately, but it's good when it does come then. I don't try to remember something that I remembered earlier on. If I'm sitting on the bus and the dialogue is running smoothly, there's a little bit of me thinks: yeah, when I'm sitting at the typewriter I hope this comes as easily. But I can't tell myself to hold on to it and then write it later.

And what about your plots, do they come as easily?

I think from the plots of the books, I would say that you get an attitude towards life that you feel this is how life might end. And in mine, it's usually a disaster like a car crash. But that's an attitude which you programme yourself at an early stage and you're probably fighting against it. You try to convince yourself that you're right all the time. Life is like this. Life is a disaster. But what is ending up good? Ending up good means that it continues, life goes on. You could just say 'they lived happily ever after.' I suppose I'm getting to the point where eventually that will happen.

Your titles – *A Streak of Madness*, *Gone in the Head*, *Ladybird in a Loony-bin* – suggest an interest in madness. Do you think you might be mad yourself?

Yes, I think that probably I have got a streak of madness myself. But I think that when a person really feels that they're mad is when they can't let their mad feelings be known. I'm sure I've talked to other people and they wonder . . . they think: am I the only person who's feeling this feeling? Part of the reason for those titles really is that, that we all know we've got mad feelings, or what society would consider to be mad. But if it's brought out in a book it isn't so bad. You're looking at another mad person, the person in the book, rather than at feelings that are really in yourself. We've all got mad feelings. Sometimes I feel hysterical.

Some of your characters are pretty crazy too.

I probably build them up, from lots of feelings that I know and lots of other people. My characters are all a combination of all the people that I know. I'm sure I could go further in a madder way; but I'm not too sure that any of my characters are really that mad. I think that if you're writing about so many characters, you'll tend to bring little bits in which come from other people or from yourself. I could be any character in any of my books.

It says here – this is the blurb on the Penguin edition of *A Streak of Madness* – you've 'had an interesting past.' What does that mean?

Does it say that? I suppose I've done a lot of jobs. When I left school I worked in a factory, then I worked in a garage and then I worked in a light engineering firm in Belfast. Then I went to college in London, studying what they called 'musical instrument technology.' Then I was a telephonist, I tried telephone business selling – toilet paper, fish. Lots of different jobs. When I was first published, I was working in the civil service. I started off being a porter, but I had a lot of trouble there and they considered that I was capable of something different, so I got promoted into the office. I had no idea what I was doing. I was there for about a year. Then I went and had a GPO training to become a telephonist. I didn't go there either because I was busy writing, so I carried on writing and got the sack.

Do you write every day?

Sometimes I do. Sometimes I get spurts of inspiration, and sometimes I try and go on a routine. If I write every day it's because I'm quite close to what I wrote the night before and I want to get back to it. I don't only work during the day. Sometimes I work all night.

You mentioned earlier that you used to teach. Do you think writing is something that can be taught?

I think some sort of writing is writing that can be taught. I don't know about writing fiction or a novel though. In my experience of teaching at night school, the people who do well are the people who can say, 'Yeah, I knew that.' I'm not saying it's not a benefit because they might be really good writers and not know that they're good writers.

So it's not a complete waste of time?

Er . . . I think people can learn to write, even fiction, but it's not so real, not so natural. They might be able to sell it, and they might be able to do quite well, but they're not natural writers.

Do you think your own writing is natural?

Yes.

And will it last?

I don't know. I don't think there's any great philosophy behind it. There's probably insight in it. I'm not too sure. It doesn't really concern me. I don't feel I'm offering a great deal to the human race. I feel I've probably got more to offer but whether it'll last more than what I've done, I can't really say. I would be pleased if it lasted, but I've got my doubts about that. I don't aim to be all that worthwhile; it's just something you do. It would be quite a pleasant way of existing if you could exist on it.

Ah, but can you exist on it? Because although you've had six novels published, three of which will be out in paperback this year, I gather you're still on the dole. Why do you go on writing?

I suppose I want to write, and if I was doing an ordinary nine to five job I'd probably write as well. I don't like working particularly, though sometimes I feel as if I'd like to do something manual. If writers are successful, they're okay. Some books sell well, they latch on. So you can't really say, I won't write a novel because after I write it I might still be on the dole. If you started off with that point of view, you probably wouldn't write at all. I would go on writing even if it meant living in poverty, but I don't think that supports my writing. I think it would be good if I could be really rich.

AFTERWORD

As a writer, Ian Cochrane is best remembered today – when remembered at all – for the impressive run of six critically acclaimed novels he produced over a ten-year period (1973-1983). But it was in the short-story format, a little earlier, that he had first made a name for himself, securing inclusion in two prestigious anthologies of new writing compiled by Faber & Faber (1971) and Penguin (1972).

Cochrane may have appeared to be an overnight success, but the reality, inevitably, was rather different. Since moving to London from his native Northern Ireland in 1959, he had dabbled in fiction for his own amusement. He later recalled how he would write in the evenings after work, often continuing through the night when the mood took him. Sub-letting his rented room for a short period, he returned to find many of his possessions missing, including his typewriter and a suitcase containing three years' worth of writing. With characteristic forbearance and self-deprecation, he later laughed off the incident, remarking that 'maybe it wasn't even worth keeping anyway . . . perhaps it wasn't a great loss.' Not daunted, Cochrane began again from scratch, patiently honing the distinctive, conversational voice of his fiction, until finally, towards the end of the 1960s, he felt ready to approach publishers with his stories, all of which drew, for both setting and idiom, on his childhood in rural Antrim.

Born in 1941, Cochrane was one of five children raised in a remote two-room cottage in Moylarg, several miles from the small village of Cullybackey. His tiny local school at Tullygrawley happened to be presided over by a most unusual master, R.L. Russell, who throughout his career challenged the rote-learning educational practices taken for granted at the time, encouraging his pupils instead to express themselves through art and writing. Creative composition in both poetry and prose was a key activity in his classroom. As set out in Russell's book, *The Child and his Pencil* (1935), the aim was to foster the pupil's 'natural freedom of expression and originality', and to 'teach writing as a living art', with a deliberate lack of emphasis on 'correct spelling and grammar and other tomfool restrictions.' Russell memorably asserted that 'error is the beginning of art, and corrections are the end of it.'

Cochrane's attendance was by all accounts sporadic – he often preferred to fish in the twisting, fast-flowing river Maine or roam the open countryside – yet Russell's nurturing of self-belief and insistence on the validity of one's local surroundings and experiences as worthy subjects for artistic depiction undoubtedly stuck with him, and he would later frequently acknowledge his schoolmaster as a formative influence and inspiration, reflecting that, 'I like to think I write the way he would have wanted me to write – down to earth stories about country life.'

At fourteen, Cochrane left school and began work at the local linen mill, enduring ten-hour shifts of heavy lifting in the bleaching department with 'water dripping on me all day.' The position proved short-lived. Cochrane, as he would have been the first to admit, was never quite able to take paid employment seriously, and his teenage years were a time of restless movement from job to job – as a stable-boy working with racehorses, an apprentice car mechanic, a hearse driver . . .

These years were also a time of significant changes and challenges. In the mid-1950s, the family moved from the countryside proper, with all its hardships and remoteness, to a four-bedroom council house in the newly built estate of Ard-na-Maine in Cullybackey. This was a pivotal moment, reflecting the wider post-war transition from traditional rural lifestyles towards a more planned urban or peri-urban existence. For the Cochrane family, the move provided long-overdue access to modern conveniences, yet came with an inevitable sense of displacement and disorientation. This relocation, Cochrane's own version of the 'trek from the land' identified by John Wilson Foster as a 'constant theme in Irish fiction', is given a central place in much of Cochrane's work, his narrators often being forced to grapple with the implications of a similar upheaval alongside the customary trials of teenage development.

It was also around this time that Cochrane began to detect a deterioration in his eyesight. While working (briefly, of course) as a petrol-pump attendant, he noticed that the dial was increasingly indecipherable, the clock on nearby Main Street a worrying blur. His vision worsened to the extent that experimental surgery was carried out in Belfast – a procedure which proved not only futile, but caused further, irreparable damage. Only much later in life would the specific condition be identified as Leber hereditary optic neuropathy, a rare genetic disorder also subsequently suffered by Cochrane's brother Drew.

He now set about learning Braille, fearing the onset of total blindness – although the illness would thankfully never develop quite to that stage – and attended a residential course in Torquay designed to teach occupational skills to the partially sighted. Then, at the age of eighteen, determined to avoid a restricted future in a small village, Cochrane made the bold decision to move to London. He accepted the opportunity to take a course in piano-tuning, a profession then considered ideal for the visually impaired. His intention to escape his apparent destiny and live life to the full was signalled as he waved goodbye to his social worker from the rail of the Belfast ferry and, according to his own account, promptly launched his white stick into the Irish Sea.

Having duly studied 'musical instrument technology' at Shoreditch Technical Institute, he found employment with a piano-tuning firm but was quickly deemed unsuited to the task and delegated to tea-making duties. This was another briefly held position. Throughout the 1960s in

London, just as he had done as a teenager in Cullybackey, Cochrane flitted from job to job at a dizzying pace. Roles as a lift attendant, addiction counsellor, domestic cleaner, telephone sales agent, and switchboard operator followed in fairly rapid succession.

Towards the end of the 1960s, while employed as a porter at the Ministry of Public Works, a disciplinary meeting following an altercation with a fellow employee resulted not in his dismissal, as he had expected, but in promotion to his own little out-of-the-way office, complete with pot plant, telephone and typewriter. His duties were never explained, and the phone never rang, but the typewriter was called into action. Cochrane was now attending a class in creative writing at Morley College in Lambeth, and his freedom from any apparent responsibilities during working hours allowed him to devote the entire day to his true passion. At Morley, his striking narrative style and original voice were soon recognised, and his first published story, 'The Hawk', appeared in the college magazine in January 1970. A close friendship with literary patron Rosey Pool, who gifted him a replacement for his stolen typewriter, brought him further connections and recommendations in the publishing world, and helped secure the appearance of his earliest stories in Faber's *Introduction 4: Stories by New Writers* (1971) and Penguin's *Modern Stories 12* (1972).

These were high-profile anthologies, inclusion in which brought immediate cachet in British literary circles. Both collections were widely reviewed, and Cochrane's contributions were often given special praise and attention, critics welcoming his 'total lack of moralising or manipulation' and 'artfully artless child's-eye delivery' (*Irish Press*). Enthusiasts included a young Derek Mahon in the *Listener*, but it was Christopher Wordsworth in the *Guardian* who perhaps did most to pave the way for Cochrane's subsequent publishing prospects by declaring, 'if the finger of the future does not single out Ian Cochrane – solid, earthy and something more [. . .] – I am no prophet'.

Thematically and stylistically, these early stories lay the groundwork for the novels which were to follow. Mental instability, religious gullibility and naive sexuality are recurring tropes, balanced by an irreverent humour never far from the surface; grotesque characterisation, similarly, is employed as much for laughs as for dramatic effect. Cochrane's loose, freewheeling but pared-back style is already in evidence too. As in his later works, jarring constructions abound, true to local speech ('I had only a thin pair of shoes with holes in them on'), as do mixed-tense phrases ('he took out his handkerchief and wipes his nose'). The overall feel is one of authenticity, of a natural story-telling voice.

All but one of the stories collected in this volume – in common with all of Cochrane's novels – are told in the first person, and from the perspective of a youthful narrator. Having a child or adolescent tell the tale directly, in a compellingly unfiltered manner, offered the ideal vehicle for sending up the flaws and pretences of the adult world. Cochrane's recurring use of a first-person, vernacular voice deliberately tightened the focus to provide an intense and often claustrophobic effect upon which the originality of his work partly hinged, yet this same approach unavoidably narrowed the possibilities of his stylistic range and authorial expression. Throughout his career, these self-imposed limitations, and the need, perhaps, to move on stylistically in subsequent work, were often highlighted by reviewers, even those otherwise greatly impressed by his latest offerings.

'The Wet Eye', one of Cochrane's most accomplished short stories, was written especially for the *Best Irish Stories* collection compiled by David Marcus in 1975. Marcus, the energetic literary anthologist and critic long associated with the *Irish Press*, was one of Cochrane's few champions in Ireland. A recurring hesitancy among cultural commentators and programmers as to how Cochrane might fit into the Irish literary landscape stemmed in no small part from the accident of his heritage. Cochrane, of course, happened to be a Northern Irish Protestant, although he set little store by religious affiliation or national identity, and throughout his life was keen to avoid being pigeonholed either personally or professionally.

Yet while he made London his home, his writing focussed relentlessly on the Bible-belt of the north-Antrim hinterlands, naturally rich in source material, under-explored and ripe for literary exploitation. Indeed, his fictional world is, in large part, resolutely local and confined, framed by a deliberately constricted outlook. In Cochrane country, the villagers seem entirely unaware of the strangeness of their existence, oblivious to any possibility that things might be done, or life might be lived, differently elsewhere. While his depiction of this distinctive locale is often a negative one – a place of emotional inarticulacy, moral disorientation and irrational violence – there can be no question of his ultimate empathy for the characters condemned to inhabit this closed space.

Cochrane undoubtedly broke new ground in terms of the Ulster Protestant literary imagination and can justly be celebrated as such. His work eschews the frequently more formal idiom and earnest intentions of predecessors such as Forrest Reid or Sam Hanna Bell to introduce elements of the surreal, the grotesque and the crude. Yet for all his innovation, Cochrane's vernacular narrative is rooted quite naturally in the non-literary, conversational style of the rural Ulster-Scots community, often perceived as pious and uptight, but in fact frequently characterised by a fondness for much that is uninhibited and 'bawdy', even deliberately outrageous and shocking, all underpinned by a sceptical worldview finding expression in dark humour. Cochrane's voice, then, is recognisably that of a Cullybackey man telling a story in intimate company; his real achievement was to channel this cultural acquisition so successfully into a literary format. Many reviewers marvelled at this clever author's ability to stay so convincingly in character throughout the length of an entire novel, perhaps little realising the extent of Cochrane's insider status. Without detracting from the skill and sophistication of Cochrane's practice, this was, to a very large degree, his own voice, rather than the projection of some gifted imitator.

All this was very much in keeping with Cochrane's

own view of himself as a 'natural' writer, one guided by inspiration and impulse, refusing to overly plan his work in advance, happily relinquishing control to his own characters. In his unpublished booklet *A New Insight into Creative Writing*, he maintained that 'the natural flow of your feelings is much more important than any elaborate descriptions that are forced.' 'Your imagination should move fast and freely,' and writers should avoid overthinking and simply get on with it, since 'if you have a story to tell, it will construct itself naturally.' 'Stop looking for the voice,' Cochrane advised, 'because you are the voice.'

And Cochrane's own practice of writing was never overly precious. If his beloved telephone rang in the middle of his creative flow, he would readily down tools and chat at length. Never tormented by the quest for the perfect sentence, he was happy to make any revisions asked of him, once remarking with typical modesty that when editors judged something to be 'not very well written' he 'tended to agree with them.' His relaxed approach also included an inclination, upon reaching a certain wordcount, to round things off with a flourish – often a car crash or other fatal occurrence – even at the risk of melodrama. And, once written, Cochrane half-joked that he never wanted to think about his work again. 'When I finish a book, I feel as if I've just had an ulcer removed,' he once explained. 'When I'm asked to talk about it afterwards, I feel as if the ulcer has just been replaced.'

*

The 1970s and early 1980s were Cochrane's heyday. Now able to write full-time, his first two novels in particular, *A Streak of Madness* (1973) and *Gone in the Head* (1974), won him great adulation, with critics rhapsodising on his 'extraordinary fidelity of observation' and 'packed and jumpy prose, full of sensations and surprises' (*TLS*). Comparisons with Salinger were made, and his fiction was proclaimed as nothing less than 'the creation of an extraordinarily gifted artist' (*Listener*). Recognition also came in the form of runner-up spot in the 1974 *Guardian* Fiction Prize for *Gone in the Head* (pipped by Beryl Bainbridge's *The Bottle Factory Outing*). Publishers and agents came and went, but half a dozen novels made their way to bookshop shelves in the space of a decade. The 1970s were also the years of his marriage to Maggie Ogilvie, providing a sense of security and routine conducive to his creative focus. *Jesus on a Stick* (1975), again set in small-town Ulster, evinced a new level of disturbing insight and well-executed ribald humour, *Ladybird in a Loony-bin* (1978) explored mental illness with a greater sense of experimentation and ambition than previously attempted, and the slim *F for Ferg* (1980) marked a strong return to the general atmosphere and setting of Cochrane's first two novels, arguably with greater poise and precision than before. Cochrane's final novel, *The Slipstream*, appeared in 1983, and stands up well as an entertaining, deliberately aimless tale of unemployed chancers adrift in West London bedsit land.

Significantly, *The Slipstream* marked out new imaginative territory, and London henceforth became the geographical focus of his fiction. For the remaining two decades of his life, Cochrane, very much a creature of habit, divided his time between his writing desk at home in St. Stephen's Gardens and the Churchill Arms pub on Kensington Church Street. Yet despite continuing to write on a quasi-daily basis, drawn as he always had been to the therapeutic benefits of the act itself, he was never able to find a publisher for either of the two novels produced during this time, *The Burning* and *A Little Red Brick*. Weighing in at 401 and 555 pages respectively, these books comprise a greater word count than all the published works taken together. And they represent something of a departure not just in their length – many of Cochrane's previous works being closer to novellas than novels – but also in the relatively mature voice of their now grown-up narrators.

Cochrane's later years, then, were a time of some disappointments. His inability to bring his work to print seemed to reflect a new climate in the British publishing industry, now more profit-focussed than editorially driven, creating an inhospitable environment for less obviously marketable material. Several mooted TV or cinema adaptations of his novels took up much of his energy but ultimately came to nothing. He also worked on a short guide to creative writing (never published) and harboured an unrealised plan to compile a collection of his short fiction. His last published story was 'Justice' (1986), in which, unusually, he explores the issue of Northern Irish sectarianism as a central theme, the Troubles previously having been little more than a distant rumbling in his work. Fittingly, this final story appeared in *More Magazine*, the literary review of Morley College, where his career in print had first begun.

Frustratingly, as Cochrane's star waned, other Irish writers came to the fore with stories of childhood and adolescence, similar in some ways to Cochrane's books, yet much more successfully marketed and received, such as Bernard MacLaverty's *Cal* and *Lamb* or Roddy Doyle's Booker Prize winning *Paddy Clarke Ha Ha Ha.* And with *The Butcher Boy*, Patrick McCabe took an anarchic, Cochranesque vision of Irish village life and injected his own manic energy and unbridled humour to create one of the great Irish novels of recent times. McCabe, indeed, has generously acknowledged the influence of Cochrane's voice on this seminal work.

But these later years were also a time of new joys and focusses, particularly through his role as 'nanny' to his ex-wife's daughter Charlotte, born in 1987, to whom in his devotion he composed stories of bees at the seaside, warring insects, and mysterious creatures lost in the mountains. And, of course, his own everyday writing continued unabated, regardless of the diminishing chances of publication. The novel *A Little Red Brick*, in particular, was ceaselessly worked and reworked over the course of more than two decades. A close friend supplying Cochrane with paper liberated from his office remembers him 'getting through reams of the stuff.' Cochrane loved to hear his great pal, and occasional actor, Imelda Kelly read extracts aloud in the Churchill Arms, and the ever-expanding tome was dispatched to publisher after publisher. Apologetic rejection letters praised the book as 'near-to-the-bone in an original, unexpected and truthful way,' while lamenting its 'disjointed' nature. But the practice of writing retained all its importance as a vital therapeutic activity. Cochrane had often noted his feeling of unease, even ill-health, if he went more than a few days without recourse to pen or keyboard, and he described his happiest moments as the hours spent hard at work at the little wooden desk in his top-floor living room, warmed by the gas fire, rain beating against the windows, surrounded by books, paintings and plants, blissfully engrossed in his fictional world.

Upon his death in 2004, at the age of just 62, Cochrane's obituarists commonly regretted the extent to which his work had fallen from view and the fact that his books were now so long out of print. Yet it was only in 2016 that something of a revival began, when QUB academic James Greer published a compelling biographical article on Cochrane via the Culture Northern Ireland website. This was followed in 2018 by a reissue of Cochrane's novel *F for Ferg*, accompanied by a panel discussion at the Seamus Heaney HomePlace celebrating Cochrane's life and legacy.

Among those who spoke at this event was Ballymena-born author Jan Carson, now at the forefront of a new wave of Northern Irish writers. Carson has noted how Cochrane's books inspired her to develop her own fictional voice, rooted in their shared native environment. 'One of the things I love about Ian's work,' she says, 'is that

I can actually hear the language coming across in it – it sounds like me, the way people like me talk.' Discovering Cochrane's fictional exploration of so much that was familiar to her helped give her the confidence to explore her own lived experience on the page. Bringing us full circle, Carson's 2022 novel *The Raptures* provides her own compelling take on what might be referred to as 'Cochrane country' – a tight-knit Antrim village in many ways similar to the enclosed world Ian Cochrane so evocatively exposed in his fiction.

Philip Taylor